TWO-GUN DEPUTY

William Colt MacDonald

Chivers Press • Thorndike Press
Bath, England • Waterville, Maine USA

This Large Print edition is published by Chivers Press, England, and by Thorndike Press, USA.

Published in 2002 in the U.K. by arrangement with the author c/o Golden West Literary Agency.

Published in 2002 in the U.S. by arrangement with Golden West Literary Agency.

U.K. Hardcover ISBN 0–7540–4843–8 (Chivers Large Print)
U.K. Softcover   ISBN 0–7540–4844–6 (Camden Large Print)
U.S. Softcover   ISBN 0–7862–3936–0 (Nightingale Series Edition)

The text of this Large Print edition is unabridged.
Other aspects of the book may vary from the original edition.

Set in 16 pt. New Times Roman.

Printed in Great Britain on acid-free paper.

British Library Cataloguing in Publication Data available

Library of Congress Cataloging-in-Publication Data

MacDonald, William Colt, 1891–1968.
　　[Deputy of Carabina]
　　　Two-gun deputy / William Colt MacDonald.
　　　　　p.　　cm.
　　　ISBN 0–7862–3936–0 (lg. print : sc : alk. paper)
　　　1. Large type books. I. Title.
　　PS3525.A2122 D46 2002
　　813'.52—dc21   2001058472

CHAPTER ONE

Five men sat around a varnish-scarred table in the Red Toro Saloon in a small cow town in southern New Mexico. It was the *siesta* hour, a period when a drowsy hush appears to prohibit all activity. Out of doors, the broiling afternoon sun beat down with fierce intensity, starting the pitch bubbling from the rough board sidewalks and warping the boards on frame shacks.

Occasionally, a vagrant breeze from the surrounding semi-desert country lifted the dust of the roadway in tiny whirling clouds that swept in through the open doorway of the Red Toro, to settle in the throats of the poker players and, consequently, increase business in the saloon. Now and then, the men at the card-table spoke brief, low-toned words, pertaining to the cards in their hands, or the pile of silver and bills heaped in the center of the table. Flies droned lazily above their heads. There weren't any other customers in the saloon.

Behind the long, rough board counter, a fat-jowled bartender with wide-open, snoring mouth, leaned against the end wall in a tilted chair, and dreamed of former days when a barkeep wore a white coat and served tall, cool, mixed drinks instead of the straight whiskey or luke-warm beer common to this small cow settlement.

Of the five players at the table, two were plainly cattlemen—lean, grizzled old-timers who fairly reeked of the raising of beef stock. One of them was Uncle Hoddy Daniels, owner of the HD Ranch. The other, old Pop Cantrell, operated the Rafter-C outfit and was also the proprietor of the town's general store.

At Cantrell's left elbow sat an individual known about town as Deuce Taggert, who had all of the earmarks of a professional gambler, though Taggert claimed he never played except for 'the fun of the game.' He was a slimly built man with shifty eyes, a lantern jaw and a reputation for a fast draw from under his arm.

Across from Taggert was seated Dobe Liston, Taggert's partner. However, there was nothing of the gambler in Liston's appearance. He was a bulkily built man with a narrow forehead, heavy brows and high cheekbones. Judged by his clothing, Liston might have been a cowpuncher—but he wasn't. He had never held a steady job, so far as anyone in town knew, yet he always appeared to possess plenty of money. It was commencing to be whispered about that Liston acted as a sort of bodyguard for Deuce Taggert.

It was the fifth player who had aroused the greatest interest in the town. Men called him the Dancer. His name actually was Jim Dance, and by coincidence his name suggested the way he walked—quick, light-stepping, with certain lithe movements that said much for his superb physical condition. Certainly, his nickname had nothing to do with any particular ability as a dancer. So far as was known, he had never entered the local dance hall—much to the regret of the girls who entertained there.

The Dancer—as he was referred to—was a rather silent individual with gray eyes and crow-black hair. His nose was straight above the small dark mustache that adorned his upper lip. He might have been thirty years of age. He was sinewy-jawed, bronzed of skin, direct of gaze.

Jim Dance, too, might have been taken for one of the local cowboys, if one were to judge by his togs—high-heeled cowboy boots, gray corduroys with wide upturned cuffs, dark-blue woolen shirt and unbuttoned vest. A scarlet bandanna was knotted at his throat and on the back of his head was placed a roll-brim black Stetson sombrero.

Twin cartridge belts criss-crossed the Dancer's slim hips, each supporting a holstered gun of forty-five calibre. It was those twin six-shooters that made men wonder. The wearing of two six-shooters, in that country, was mostly confined to outlaws or law officers. The Dancer didn't seem to be either, so far as the town could make out. Neither did he have any visible means of support. He lived at the small ramshackle hotel, kept a roan gelding at the local livery stable, asked no unseemly questions and imparted not the least information regarding his own activities. All of this aroused the town's curiosity to no small extent. The Dancer was, in short, something of a mystery in that small settlement—an unsolved mystery.

There was some conversation among the card players, now, following a long period of almost unbroken silence. A few moments later, Deuce Taggert laughed shortly, put down his cards, face up, and raked in the money from the center of the table. Dobe Liston turned in his chair, called an order to the sleeping bartender whose name was Curly. Drinks were served. Old Pop Cantrell growled something about his 'cursed luck.' Uncle Hoddy Daniels nodded agreement without speaking. Dobe Liston agreed that it was 'too bad' the cards hadn't run better for Pop.

Taggert laughed again, then feeling the Dancer's eyes on him, sobered abruptly and picked up his drink. The Dancer remained silent.

Taggert reached for the cards, began to shuffle them deftly between his quick fingers. 'It's my deal, gentlemen,' he commented. 'I'll try to give the heavy losers the sort of pasteboards they're craving, this time.'

Feeling Jim Dance's gaze still on him, he slowed his shuffling as though to show there

4

was nothing underhanded in the motions. The Dancer smiled slightly. After a moment, Taggert put down the cards in front of old Pop Cantrell to be cut. 'Cut 'em, Pop,' Taggert said.

Pop reached over, lifted the top half of the deck so that Taggert might rearrange the two portions.

'Hold it, Pop,' the Dancer commanded softly.

'Huh?' Old Pop looked up in surprise, then placed the cards back to their original position. 'What's the matter, Jim?'

'I don't reckon we'd better go on with this game,' the Dancer said quietly.

'What's the matter?' Dobe Liston grunted. 'You weary of playin'?'

'I don't like those cards,' the Dancer said in his soft even tones.

Taggert frowned. 'You mean you want a new deck?'

'I didn't say that,' the Dancer drawled.

Something in Jim Dance's manner made Taggert nervous. 'Look here, Dance,' Taggert said testily, 'you objected to further play, just when *I* was commencing to deal. Don't you like the way I deal 'em out?'

The Dancer repeated, 'I didn't say that.'

'Well for the love of little rattlesnake puppies,' old Pop Cantrell growled, 'why don't you say what's wrong, Dancer. We're willin' to do anythin' to please, but if you won't state yore trouble, we ain't mind-readers and can't help you out none.'

Dance explained, 'I don't like playing with marked cards.' His voice was steady, calm—and at the same time, accusing.

'Marked cards!' Uncle Hoddy exclaimed. He glanced quickly at the others, his face slowly growing red.

'You're crazy!' Liston snapped.

Taggert said angrily, 'Where'd you get that idea, Dance? We're all friends here. You've said too much to stop now. I demand an explanation.'

The Dancer turned the cards face down on the table. On the back of each card was printed an ordinary diamond-mesh design, in blue ink against a white background. Quickly he pointed out certain faint, almost indiscernible blue shadings against the white of the design of some of the cards. 'It's plain as the rattles on a diamond-back, when you know what to look for,' he said softly. 'Look here . . . and here . . . and here . . . Here's another. Notice how those blue lines look sort of blurred—?'

There was a quick intake of breath from Pop Cantrell. Uncle Hoddy swore an oath of mingled surprise and anger. Dobe Liston remained silent, as though waiting for Deuce Taggert to speak up.

Taggert's laughter sounded forced when it came, even though it was intended to appear scornful. 'The joke's on you, Dance,' he sneered. 'Those ain't marked cards. I see what you mean by the design being blurred thataway. But that's probably the fault of the company that manufactures them. It's a printing error, I'd say. Maybe the plates slipped when these cards were being run through, or the printer might have had some ink on his hands and smeared—'

'And smeared said ink on just the face cards and aces, eh?' The Dancer's words sounded humorous, but they weren't. 'How come, Taggert, that you know so much about the printing of playing cards?'

Taggert's eyes widened. He started to speak, then checked the words as he rose half-way from his chair. Abruptly, his right hand darted inside his open coat!

Dance made his draw without rising. To the others at the table, it looked as though the gun had appeared in his hand by magic. He fired once only, but the hammer fell on his cartridge before Taggert's gun-barrel had cleared its underarm holster!

Taggert stumbled back, overturning his chair. His gun clattered to the floor. The others were on their feet now. Dobe Liston was clawing at his holster.

'Hold it, Liston!' the Dancer said sternly. His other gun was out now, covering Dobe Liston.

Liston gave a frightened gasp, released the

7

grip on his gun and jerked both hands in the air.

'Well, I'll be damned!' Uncle Hoddy exclaimed.

'Get their guns, Uncle Hoddy—Pop,' the Dancer spoke quickly. 'Then take a look at Taggert. I don't figure he's bad hurt.'

Taggert was already climbing to his feet. He stumbled half-erect and dropped weakly into his chair which old Pop shoved behind him. The right sleeve of Taggert's coat was bullet-slashed. Blood dripped from his finger-tips. He slumped down, pale as death, head hanging, without a single word. Then he asked for a doctor. He demanded, too, that Curly go for the town marshal to arrest the Dancer.

'Marshal's up north, visitin' his mother,' Curly gave the information. 'The sheriff's takin' his place today—'

'Dammit,' Taggert groaned; 'go get the sheriff.'

Curly looked uncertainly at the Dancer. The Dancer shook his head. 'I reckon Brite's on his way here, now, if he heard the shot.'

'Well, there's been powder exploded,' Uncle Hoddy commented, 'but I don't yet see any proof these cards was marked—'

Old Pop Cantrell cut in grimly, 'Taggert's goin' for his gun proves he is guilty. At the same time, I just don't see—'

His words were cut short by the sounds of running feet outside. The citizenry, called by

8

the sound of the shot, was arriving to investigate. A crowd of men gathered at the entrance, pushed on inside the saloon. A tall, white-haired man, wearing a sheriff's star, came shoving through the press of humanity at the doorway. He was Sheriff Brite Mason.

The Dancer explained what had happened and his story was reenforced by details from Curly, old Pop and Uncle Hoddy. Dobe Liston maintained a sullen silence. Taggert refused to open his mouth, beyond asking that someone run for a doctor.

The white-haired sheriff turned quizzical eyes on the Dancer. 'I reckon,' he drawled, 'that I won't attempt to hold you, Jim, for this shootin'. To all appearances it was done in self-defence. Taggert's actions proves him guilty. At the same time, I just don't savvy how you figured out he marked these cards.'

The Dancer smiled, moved around the table in quick easy steps to reach the side of the trembling Taggert. One lean bronzed hand slipped quickly into the side pocket of Taggert's coat. Taggert started to resist, then groaned loudly as he lifted his wounded arm.

'Here 'tis,' the Dancer said, drawing from the gambler's pocket a small round ball, coloured blue. 'Beeswax,' the Dancer explained. 'Taggert soaked it in some sort of blue dye that coloured one finger whenever he touched it. Look . . .'

The Dancer drew one finger across the

small ball, then passed his finger lightly across the back of one of the marked cards, making a second mark which closely resembled a printing blemish. Then Dance held up the card for inspection.

An angry gasp of complete surprise broke from the spectators' lips.

Now, Dance held up for inspection the finger that had made the mark. It showed not the slightest trace of the blue dye. 'See,' he went on, 'it doesn't leave any stain on a finger. All of the dye comes off on the cards. Only the slightest touch is necessary to mark a card this way. No, it wasn't necessary for Taggert to buy cards already marked from some crook. He marked his own as he went along, after a game had started. Maybe you've all noticed that he's never objected to opening a brand-new deck. Now you know why. After he's played a few hands, he has the pasteboards all marked to suit his own convenience. Well, have I proved the truth of my statements?'

'Yo're tootin' damn right!' old Pop Cantrell burst out.

'Full and complete,' Uncle Hoddy nodded, eyeing Taggert angrily.

While the men were still talking, Dobe Liston took advantage of the situation to make his escape outside.

The sheriff ordered the crowd to depart and in a short time, excepting the sheriff, only the original occupants of the saloon remained inside.

Badly frightened by this time, Taggert agreed to go with the sheriff. A crowd outside followed the pair to the jail, hooting and calling down maledictions on Taggert's head.

In the saloon were left only Curly, Uncle Hoddy, old Pop Cantrell and Jim Dance. Uncle Hoddy ordered drinks for the three of them, as they lined up at the bar, then asked, 'How 'bout it, Dancer, you aimin' to prefer charges agin Taggert? You know we got a town ordinance agin tinhorn gamblers—'

'I'll have to think that over,' Dance replied. 'Offhand, I'd say "no". I think it would be best to order him out of town. There's no need putting your county to the expense of keeping him in jail.'

'We-ell,' Uncle Hoddy said slowly, 'I sort of reckon yo're right.'

'I try to be right,' Dance smiled. Within a few moments he finished his drink, said *adiós* and departed for the street.

When the Dancer was out of sight, Uncle Hoddy said, 'The Dancer is a dang nice cuss— but sort of queer like. I can't figure him out, nohow. How long has he been hanging around town, Curly?'

The bartender considered the question. ' 'Bout a month now, I reckon,' Curly said finally. 'Dance and another feller named Newport arrived in town together. Newport only stayed 'bout three-four days, then moved

11

on. I don't know where, and the Dancer ain't never told me. And he's the sort of hombre you hesitate to ask questions of.'

'Ain't that the truth.' Uncle Hoddy nodded. 'When did Taggert and Dobe Liston first arrive here in these parts?'

More furrowing of Curly's brow, then, 'Around five weeks back.'

Old Pop Cantrell broke in, 'Hoddy, you sort of figuring the Dancer is keeping Taggert's trail warm?'

'Don't it look that way?'

Pop nodded thoughtfully. 'Yeah, it does, at that. But if Jim Dance is a law officer, why don't he take Taggert up?'

'You needn't to ask me,' Uncle Hoddy said querulously. 'I've nigh to wore my brain in shreds already, tryin' to figure out the Dancer.'

CHAPTER TWO

From the Red Toro Saloon, the Dancer walked to Sheriff Brite Mason's office. For the next fifteen minutes he talked steadily to the sheriff. At the end of that period, the sheriff nodded agreement to certain plans outlined by Dance, then retired to the jail cells at the rear of his office. Dance waited in the sheriff's office.

Within a few minutes, the sheriff returned.

The Dancer rose and stepped out to the street, Brite Mason at his heels. On the sidewalk, the sheriff asked, 'I suppose you ain't no objections, Dance, if I release Taggert in time for him to catch the five-forty train when it comes through?'

Dance consulted his watch. He looked up. 'Did Taggert say he wanted to catch the five-forty?'

Brite Mason nodded. 'Didn't say where he intended heading, though. I asked, but he said he wa'n't certain where he'd go. Mebbe he just wants to get out of town pronto, before somebody he's cheated at cards mows him down . . . The five-forty is the next train, though, today.'

'The train west,' Dance mused. 'He's aiming to head west. . . . Yes,' to the sheriff, 'let him catch the five-forty. Better let him out, right away. I want to see what he does, around town.'

Mason nodded. 'I'll do that, Dancer. Anything else?'

'Nothing I can think of at present.'

Dance turned away, walked slowly down the street.

At a small building whose sun-faded sign announced it to be the U. S. Post Office, Dance turned and entered. Presenting himself at the window wicket, he received a letter from the wizened old postmaster. Dance didn't open the letter until he was again on the street.

Lounging in the shade before the post office, he slowly read and reread the enclosed note:

> *Dear Jim* it ran, *I'm commencing to believe you were right about Carabina. I found traces of the stuff in Bosquecito, but think it was just passing through. Our trail seems to be narrowing to something definite. I'm leaving for Carabina as soon as I mail this. Hope you've had better luck than I. Hurriedly,*
> *Frank Newport.*

Dance glanced along the street, eyes vague with speculation. 'Carabina lies west,' he was thinking. 'The five-forty travels west. Perhaps the trail *is* narrowing.'

He strode lightly along the main street of the town, which sloped gradually down toward the raised dirt platform and corrugated iron shanty which served as the local railroad depot. Across from the depot, he dropped to a seat on the hard adobe earth, his back braced against the side wall of a neighboring Mexican hut, not far from the tracks. His fingers searched for and located a sack of cigarette tobacco and papers. A moment later he was lighting his smoke and exhaling twin plumes of gray through his nostrils.

A Mexican woman emerged from the hut, saw the Dancer and called shrill crackling Spanish to someone within the house. Two Mexicans emerged, rounded the corner of the

14

house and dropped down to seats on either side of the Dancer. The woman reentered the hut.

Then Dancer nodded to the two Mexicans, waited until they had rolled corn-husk cigarettes. Finally he spoke. 'Has the sheriff released him yet?'

'*Si, señor*, right after you departed from the sheriff's office.'

'Where did he go?'

'To the *fonda*—how you say?—the hotel, no? Yes, to the hotel. He departs on the train which leaves at five-forty—or so he announced at the hotel. He paid his bill. Juan, here, made a trade for the money, when the Señor Taggert departed. The hotel clerk, he thinks we are *loco*.' The Mexican's smile flashed whitely.

Dance turned to the other Mexican who was holding out two five-dollar bills. Dance accepted them and in return gave Juan twelve silver dollars.

'*Gracias, amigo,*' Dance said softly, tucking the bills away. Then to the first Mexican, 'Where is Taggert now?'

'Pascual is watching him. After leaving the hotel, Taggert went in search of the Señor Dobe Liston. The two of them are sitting in the shade of the big oak that grows near the harness shop.'

'*Bueno.*' Dance nodded.

The three men lapsed into silence. The sun was dropping fast now. Shadows deepened

15

about the trio. Dance glanced across the street, toward the small depot. A large number of the town's citizens had gathered there to await the arrival of the daily westbound train. Dance saw Taggert and Dobe Liston climb to the dirt platform. Liston waited outside, while Taggert entered the depot. In a few minutes, Taggert reappeared and stood in earnest conversation with Liston, apart from the other men on the platform.

A train whistled two miles to the east. The crowd edged up toward the tracks. Taggert shook hands with Liston and a moment later was lost in the crowd. A slim Mexican youth appeared suddenly from the opposite side of the station, and crossed the street to join Dance and his companions.

'Comes Pascual,' Juan commented shortly.

The Mexican boy stopped before Dance and squatted on his heels in the dust. He, too, must roll and light a cigarette before indulging in conversation. Dance waited patiently.

Finally, 'It is arranged with the Señor Liston,' the Mexican boy spoke softly, 'to prevent the Dancer from leaving this town.'

'How?' Dance asked briefly.

'By the route of the gun.'

The Dancer smiled a bit wearily. 'I expected it. Cripes, won't they ever learn to try some other way?'

'Only the good *Dios* knows.'

16

At the depot, the conductor of the train was shouting his 'All abo-o-oard-d-d!' In a few moments the train got under way again, sending back swirls of white smoke and steam in a final farewell. Slowly the crowd on the platform wended its way back toward the center of town. Liston had disappeared with the rest.

The Dancer spoke to Pascual. 'What made Taggert think I intend leaving?'

'He is not sure. Just in case . . . you understand, señor? In any event, Liston is to rub you out, if possible. Those were the words of Taggert which I have overheard.'

Half to himself, Dance said, 'Is Taggert getting suspicious, or just wants me rubbed out because of what happened today?'

'He is not badly hurt, I heard him say,' Pascual went on. 'The doctor bandaged his arm under his shirt. He does not even lose the use of it for a small period.'

'What is next for us?' asked the Mexican named Mateo.

'You will stay here with your woman,' Dance told him. 'After I learn where I'm heading, I'll tell Pascual and Juan what to do.'

'*Gracias, señor.*' Mateo smiled. 'I like not over-much this leaping from town to town like a flea on the dog's spine.'

'It is right that Juan and I should watch the Liston hombre, no?' Juan asked. 'He might come from behind you and—'

17

The Dancer smiled. 'I reckon I'll be able to take care of Liston,' he said. 'After I've left it might be a good idea to keep a record of his actions, though I don't figure he knows a great deal.'

'*Si, señor.*'

The Dancer talked a few minutes longer, then arose and sauntered across to the depot which, by now, was empty of all save the station agent. Entering the corrugated iron building, Dance engaged the agent in a desultory conversation. After a time he commented idly, 'So Taggert is heading for his home in Utah, eh?'

'That so?' the agent said. 'That's queer.'

'What is?'

'I'm wondering how come he didn't buy his ticket to the end of the line then, instead of just getting one to take him to Carabina—'

'He probably had some business in Carabina.' Dance yawned.

'Mebbe so. You know, Dance, I figure Taggert was getting out on your account, more than anything else. Beating him to the shot that way, must have thrown a scare into him.'

But Dance wasn't listening. He was halfway through the doorway. 'I'll be seeing you again,' he said over his shoulder.

The sun was low now, dropping behind the peaks of the distant mountains that sprawled to the west of the town. Dusk was settling down. A chill breeze commenced to stir the air. The Dancer walked slowly back toward the center of the town. Lights were commencing to gleam from windows.

At the sheriff's office, Dance paused a moment in the open doorway. The sheriff adjusted the shade on the oil lamp on his desk and glanced up at the Dancer's soft step.

The Dancer spoke one word. 'Carabina,' he said.

'Your hunch was right, then.' Brite Mason nodded. 'When do you leave, Jim?'

'There's a freight through here just before dawn, in the morning,' Dance said. He added, 'See that my bronc is well looked after, will you, Brite? If I stay in Carabina long enough I'll send for him.'

He faded back into the darkness that had descended on the town by this time and continued along the street, until he came to his hotel.

The Dancer entered the building and found his room. He didn't light the lamp, but after removing his boots lay down on the bed to catch a few hours' sleep.

False dawn was commencing to streak the eastern horizon when Dance awakened. He sat up, donned his sombrero and commenced rolling a cigarette. With that lighted, he drew on his boots, rose and reached for his coat, after buckling on his guns again. He was ready to travel. Putting one hand in his pocket, he drew out some money and left it on the dresser

19

to pay for his room rent.

The window of his room opened quietly. The Dancer thrust one leg over the ledge, then slid outside. It was only a short drop to the earth below.

There wasn't a soul in sight when he reached the street. He headed toward the railroad station. Arriving there, he looked about him, then abruptly faded into the shadow of the darkened, corrugated iron station. Across the tracks he had spotted a pinpoint of red fire. Someone smoking a cigarette. The Dancer wondered who it was and guessed at Liston. He wondered also if the unknown smoker, if it were Liston, had seen him arrive. The glowing end of the cigarette didn't appear again.

If that is Liston, Dance mused, is he just heading for Carabina to join Taggert, or is he following me? Maybe he had a hunch I'd pull out on the freight when it came through. He's been waiting to see. Or maybe he came down to catch the freight himself.

While he stood thinking the matter over, the long drawn whistle of a locomotive sounded a mile away, around a sharp curve of the tracks. The train would have to slow up a bit to negotiate the curve. The engine must be drawing a heavy load, judging from the labored puffing sounds it made. That was good—it wouldn't be going too fast when it came through town.

Dance stiffened suddenly at a nearby sound, one hand darting toward his hip. Then he relaxed. Pascual, the Mexican youth took form in the darkness.

'*Señor*,' he whispered, 'it is Liston who waits across the tracks.'

'I figured as much. Has he been shadowing me, or does he plan to leave town?'

'That I do not know. You plan to ride the freight train?'

'*Si*, Pascual. I go to Carabina. You and Juan remain, along with Mateo. If Liston catches the train, you and Juan come to Carabina. There is no hurry, though. Keep open your eyes and ears if Liston remains here.'

'*Si*, Señor Dancer.'

The locomotive whistle sounded closer. The rails commenced to hum. Dance found Pascual's hand and pressed it hard. A white glare from the engine headlight abruptly burst around the curve in the rails. In that brief moment of illumination, Dance glanced across the tracks. No one was to be seen, but there was considerable brush growing at that point which might have concealed a man.

The train was thundering in, now. Dance broke from the cover of the railroad station darting out to the tracks. For a moment he was standing boldly in the light from the engine. Across the tracks a gun roared suddenly, savagely.

The Dancer's gun flipped out. Orange fire

21

burst from his hand. He knew he had missed. There was no particular mark to shoot at, but he was trying to spoil Liston's aim. Back of him he heard Pascual's gunfire added to his own, and like his own it was probably ineffective.

The next instant, Dance was enveloped in a cloud of steam and smoke as the locomotive roared past. He felt the heat of the engine on his face as he moved in closer. Behind the engine a long string of box cars swayed and rumbled. The Dancer awaited his opportunity. It was difficult in the darkness.

Abruptly his feet left the ground as he leaped through the air, fingers clutching at, tightening on, the iron ladder on one of the box cars. He felt the earth fall away from beneath him as he secured his hold. For a brief second his lean body was whipped viciously through the air. There was a tugging at his armpits. The rush of wind carried his body close and his feet found a foothold on the iron rungs of the ladder.

Then he was climbing to the top of the freight car. Reaching the narrow platform that ran along the top, he glanced back. A few lights shone dimly near the center of the fast receding town. That was all he could see through the swirling smoke that was blown back from the engine. He wondered if Pascual had shot Liston, or if Liston had also caught this train. Dance glanced along the roofs of the swaying cars. So far as his gaze penetrated the darkness, he could see no one. Carefully he made his way back to the caboose, at the end of the train.

CHAPTER THREE

Dance pushed open the caboose door and stepped inside the swaying car. On the cushioned seat that ran the length of the caboose sat a sleepy-eyed pair, the freight conductor and the brakeman. They glanced up in astonishment, as Dance entered and closed the door behind him. He moved toward the cushioned seat.

'Where in hell did you come from?' the conductor demanded.

'Caught your train as you came through town, back there,' Dance explained. 'I'll be dropping off at Carabina. I didn't have time to wait for the next passenger train.'

'You mean to say,' the brakeman exploded, 'that you picked us up on the run?'

'No other way to catch you.' Dance smiled cheerfully. 'It wasn't so difficult. Your engineer had slowed down for that sharp curve. Besides, you're hauling a heavy load and—'

'Ain't it right,' the conductor broke in. 'We're pulling a lot of mining machinery to be put off at Carabina.'

'Anyway,' Dance continued, 'it was easier than I figured it would be to catch you . . . Stopping at Carabina, eh? Good. I won't have to get off on the run . . . What's the fare to Carabina?'

'Forget it,' the conductor grunted. 'You're named Dance, aren't you?'

'That's it. Jim Dance.'

He leaned back on the cushioned bench. Gray light was commencing to filter through the caboose windows. The brakie fell asleep. The conductor commenced busying himself with a sheaf of papers and a lead pencil.

Clickety-click . . clickety-clack, the train sped over the rails. It was gradually growing lighter in the caboose. A shaft of golden light suddenly burst through a side window.

'Morning,' the conductor said briefly, and went back to his papers. The brakie replied with a heavy snore. The Dancer sat up straighter, yawned and stretched. He drew his right gun, plugged out an empty shell and introduced fresh ammunition into the cylinder. The conductor looked at him rather queerly, but didn't say anything.

Once, Dance asked, 'What time do we get in Carabina?'

The conductor squinted at his watch, replied, 'We'll get in about six this evening. Ordinarily we're due there about five thirty-eight, but today we've got to lay over, eight miles this side of Floresburg and let some big

24

bug's special eastbound through.'

The train jolted along across the flat, changeless, seemingly endless stretch of country. Occasionally short stops were made along the line. Now and then the freight was forced to wait on a side track while some eastbound train rushed past.

It was about two in the afternoon when the brakie returned from one of his trips outside to announce, 'We're carrying a hobo. Want I should kick him off?'

The conductor frowned. 'Criminey! Let him ride, Charley. He won't do any harm. This is bad country to be dumped off in. What's he got to say for himself?'

The brakie shook his head. 'I didn't get a chance to talk to him. I was walking the cars, up on top. I just spied his head sticking up between two boxcars. He ducked down when he saw me. He's up ahead, five or six cars.'

'Let him ride,' the conductor said.

The Dancer asked the brakeman, 'What did this hobo look like?'

'I just saw his head,' the shack replied. 'Didn't get a decent look at him. He was wearing a sombrero like the cowboys wear . . . Say, maybe he isn't a regular tramp, after all. Some busted cowhand, more'n likely.'

'Let him ride,' the conductor repeated. 'Forget him. It may be contrary to company rules, but—well, we ain't to blame for what we forget.'

The brakie nodded and dropped down on the cushioned seat. Another hour passed. The train had crossed the mountain range now and emerged on a stretch of semi-desert country. Almost as far as the eye could see, to distant mountain ranges, rolling sandhills, covered with sage and cactus, rose on either side.

Dance stared through the open rear door of the caboose at the twin ribbons of steel track unwinding from beneath the train, his mind lost in thought. He wondered if Dobe Liston had caught the train after all, or if it were really a hobo the brakie had spotted. If it was Liston, it meant that Pascual had missed his shot.

Fifteen minutes passed. Now the wheels of the train slowed and Dance saw it had left the main rails and come to a stop on a short spur. 'What now?' he asked.

'This is where we wait for that special that's headed east,' the conductor replied. 'You know, the one I mentioned this morning. We're eight miles outside of Floresburg.'

Dance followed the brakeman and conductor from the caboose and dropped to the earth. His high heels crunched on the cinders between the two sections of track. Up ahead, the waiting engine was puffing and chugging.

All around were sandhills covered with cacti and sage brush. The brakeman was walking along the length of cars, peering under each

26

one.

The conductor chuckled. 'My shack is looking for that hobo. He'll never find him. That 'bo probably dropped off and is hid in these hills. He won't come out until the train starts again.'

'How long will we be here?' Dance asked.

'Twenty minutes, anyway—maybe longer.'

Dance nodded. 'I reckon I'll take a walk and stretch my legs. I'm getting sort of cramped sitting so long.'

The Dancer turned and rounded the end of the train, then glanced up the tracks toward the engine. There was no one to be seen on this side. Thoughts ran through Dance's head. If that was Liston, he's hid behind one of these hills. Maybe I can draw his fire. If I can bring him into the open . . .

The thought remained unfinished as Dance left the tracks and strode boldly between two sandhills. For five minutes he walked on, ankle deep in sand at some spots; at others the footing was firmer. He climbed a hill and looked back toward the train. It stood as before. There was no one in sight.

The Dancer wondered if Liston were following him. Even at that moment, the man might be fitting his gun and preparing to pull trigger. Doggedly, Dance walked on, dipping into a long hollow.

Suddenly, from some distance away, he heard a train whistle. It was immediately

27

answered by the engine of the freight train.

'Cripes!' Dance whirled around. 'Time has passed faster than I figured. I'd better be getting back before I get left.'

At that instant, he saw a spurt of sand fly up at his feet and heard the report of a six-shooter. The Dancer spun, reaching for his guns. A second shot breezed past his cheek.

Back at the railroad track, the freight engine was blowing off a blast of steam. The other train sounded nearer now.

Then, just above a ridge of sand, half-hidden by a stunted mesquite bush, Dance saw Dobe Liston's head. Liston was just raising his six-shooter for a third shot. The man's eyes were red with furious anger, his lips drawn back in a hideous snarl.

Twin streams of white fire lanced out from Dance's fists, clenched about his gun-butts. The four reports, so close together, sounded almost like one. Dance heard a sharp agonized cry of pain and saw bits of mesquite twigs leap into the air, as Liston's head disappeared.

The Dancer waited but a moment more. The eastbound special was sounding still nearer now, as Dance leaped up the side of the sandhill behind which Liston had been hidden. He topped the crest, then two yards away he saw Liston sprawled awkwardly on his back. The man's eyes were already glazing in death.

The Dancer nodded grimly. 'You had the first two shots, Liston,' he said grimly. 'It was you or me.'

Thrusting the twin guns back into holsters, Dance turned and hurried back toward the freight train. While he was still a hundred yards from the tracks, the eastbound special flashed past and the freight was already starting to move off the spur. On the platform of the caboose the conductor was waving frantically for Dance to hurry.

Dance broke into a run and leaped aboard the train just as it was getting under way.

'Dam'd if I didn't think you was going to miss us,' the conductor laughed. 'That special was a few minutes sooner than I expected.' He entered the caboose, followed by Dance. Panting, Dance dropped down on the cushions and started reloading his guns. The conductor jumped to conclusions. 'Thought I heard shooting, only the trains were making so much noise, I wasn't sure. There's a heap of rattlesnakes in those hills. You must have stirred one up.'

'He stirred me up,' Dance said soberly.

'Get him?'

Dance nodded. 'He was tough, though. It took four shots.'

'You have to hit 'em just right,' the conductor said sagely.

'I reckon.'

Clickety-click . . clickety-clack, the train was gathering speed now. Two hours more would bring it into Carabina.

CHAPTER FOUR

Carabina, though it occupied the position of county seat in Rizla County, bore but lightly and with little dignity its various responsibilities. It was located in the center of a huge platter-shaped valley, midway between the Sangre de Santos Mountains on the east and Fuente Range on the west. To the south, several miles away, was the Mexican border. North of Carabina, and almost towering above it, were the Roquero Hills a tumbled mass of jagged granite on the slopes of which brush and cacti made but feeble progress.

Originally, Carabina had served principally as a source of supply and cattle shipping point for the various ranches that spread fanwise to the west, east and south of town, but with the discovery of silver in the Roquero Hills everything changed. Carabina took on the importance of a boom town, and grew by leaps and bounds. Real estate agents flourished. Three side streets were opened, parallel to the main street, and a short time later, cross streets were laid out and dwelling lots staked off and sold to gullible purchasers.

The buildings were of all sorts—adobe, frame, frame and canvas, rock and adobe. The county house was of brick; ranged on either side of it and across the street were various types of false-fronted buildings. Tinhorn gamblers operated on small tables placed along the sidewalk. Three-shell men were numerous. Saloons and gambling halls sprung into being overnight. This drew not only the riff-raff from both sides of the Mexican border, but outlaws and wanted men from other parts of the country as well.

In short, Carabina was pretty much a wide-open town, though Sheriff Sam Purdy and his deputy, Chuck Osborn, did what was possible to hold the lawless element in check. But it required more than two good law officers to hold down the murderers and thieves who were fighting to rule Carabina. More than once, Sheriff Purdy had been on the point of calling on the state militia for help, but Purdy was as stubborn as he was honest, and he believed, to use his own words, 'in washin' his dirty linen, hisself.'

Ringleaders in the crime circle that infested Carabina were Nick Grindall and Hutch Worden who owned in partnership Carabina's most notorious honkytonk, the Red Phoenix. Grindall also ran the Bow-Knot Ranch that lay twelve miles to the west of town. Grindall had sometimes been suspected of 'tossing a wide loop' where his neighbours' cows were concerned, but no proof of this fact had been forthcoming. Hutch Worden's reputation as a killer helped to keep too many people from asking questions regarding his partner's beef-raising activities. Worden's guns were notched and he never denied the shootings laid to his door, though, somehow, he always managed to prove them done in self-defense.

There had been some talk of running Grindall for mayor at the next town election. Sheriff Purdy had received this news with a grim shudder, knowing 'hell would break loose' in earnest were such a happening to come to pass. Grindall had a strong following in town and given legal authority would turn Carabina into a veritable gateway to Hades. At the same time, Purdy felt were it not for Grindall and Hutch Worden, he would have been able to hold the town with a tight rein and enforce the laws. In time, Purdy figured, the boom town spirit would pass, and Carabina again settle to a staid, respectable existence. But to get rid of Nick Grindall and Hutch Worden was easier thought of than accomplished.

Dusk was creeping in when the freight train that carried the Dancer ran on a spur and came to a stop on the outskirts of Carabina. Dance said good-bye to the conductor and brakeman, and swung down to the ground. From this point he made his way to the center of town on foot. The Dancer's face grew grim as he walked the plank sidewalks. No doubt about it, Carabina was hard. Miners, cowboys, gamblers and Mexicans thronged the streets. An almost unbroken line of ponies and wagons stood at hitch-racks on either side. The swinging doors of saloons were in continual motion. From various gambling houses came the click of poker chips or the whirring of wheels.

Dance stopped at a restaurant, ate his supper and washed it down with black coffee. With a cigarette glowing between his lips, he commenced to feel better, as he stepped again into the now-darkened street. By this time the miners were pouring down from the 'diggin's' in the Roquero Hills, and the streets were noisy with their arrival.

From the restaurant, Dance made his way to a building bearing a sign which said, THE COWMAN'S REST HOTEL. It was the usual hotel, typical of the cow and mining country— two story with a saloon and dining-room downstairs and the hotel rooms on the second floor. Here, Dance secured a room, ascended the stairs and washed up. Leaving his coat behind, he descended to the barroom, which by this time was commencing to gather customers.

The Dancer ordered a bottle of beer and, after a time, engaged the bartender in conversation. The bartender also acted as hotel clerk and seemed the logical source from which to secure certain information Dance was seeking. He was a well-spoken young fellow named Jeff Reed.

'Yes, you'll like this town all right,' Jeff

Reed said, somewhat grimly, 'if you like your towns wild. We're not doing any boasting, but we like to say the Cowman's Rest has managed to keep clean despite the sudden inrush of tough hombres. Know what I mean?'

The Dancer nodded. 'I get your slant, Reed.'

'You here on business?' Reed asked.

The Dancer said carelessly, 'I hope so. I'll have to look around a mite before I make any definite decisions.' He added, 'By the way, I sort of expected to meet a friend of mine here—man named Frank Newport.'

Jeff Reed's face brightened. 'Sure enough. Cattle buyer, isn't he?'

Dance hesitated just a moment, then, 'That's him, reckon, though there's a lot of cattle buyers floating around the country.'

'I remember the name, now. It was Frank Newport, all right. Big man with a husky pair of shoulders on him. Dark complected.'

'That's him,' Dance nodded again. 'Is he still in town? Do you know?'

Jeff Reed shook his head. 'He left four or five days ago. He stayed here at the hotel when he first came, then went out to Nick Grindall's ranch—'

'Who?'

'Nick Grindall. He runs the Bow-Knot iron, twelve miles west of town. Grindall took him out to his place to stay a couple of days, while he looked over the range and checked up to

34

see what stock Grindall had for sale.'

'Did he buy any cows?' Dance asked.

'I don't think so. Newport told me he was looking for high grade stuff. I suppose Grindall couldn't fill the bill. Anyway, Newport sent one of Grindall's men in for his baggage, with money to pay his hotel bill. He also sent me a note saying that if anyone came looking for him, to say he hadn't found what he was after. I'm not surprised. Grindall's stock don't grade very high.'

'Hadn't found what he was after, eh?' The Dancer repeated the words slowly, thoughtfully.

'That's what the note said.' Reed nodded. 'I mislaid it some place, otherwise I'd show it to you.'

Dance would have given a lot to have seen that note, but all he said was, 'It doesn't make any difference, Reed. Did Newport say where he was going?'

Reed shook his head. 'His note didn't mention it. One of Grindall's men was in here, one day, and he told me Grindall loaned Newport a horse and saddle. I gathered that Newport had headed down toward the border. He might find a few good Mex cattle down that way, at that.'

'Uh-huh, he might. By the way, how did Newport get out to the Bow-Knot?'

'Rode out in Grindall's buckboard. One of the Bow-Knot hands happened to be in town

35

for supplies.'

'Must be,' Dance speculated, 'that Newport figures to return here.'

'Well, I don't know.' Reed looked dubious. 'His note to me didn't say so.'

'You said one of Grindall's hands came in for Newport's baggage. The baggage must be at the Bow-Knot. I don't figure Newport would carry his baggage with him on horseback.'

'By gosh! That's right. Still, he might. He only had a small handbag and a coat with him.'

Dance asked next, 'What sort of hombre is this Grindall?'

Reed didn't reply at once, then he said slowly, 'I'd just as soon not say. Folks that don't speak well of Grindall have a habit of getting into trouble. I'd sooner not make any comments.'

'I understand . . . Maybe I'll find out for myself. You say the Bow-Knot is twelve miles due west of here?'

Reed nodded, adding, 'But you'll probably see Grindall around town. He and Hutch Worden own the Red Phoenix—that's a combination dancehall, saloon and gambling house, here. Grindall spends most of his time in town these days.'

A customer farther down the bar rapped for service and Reed hurried away. Dance frowned thoughtfully and headed toward the street.

A cowpuncher put down his empty glass, and said to Reed, 'Jeff, who's that hombre you were talking to?'

'I don't know much about him,' Reed replied. 'He registered with the hotel as Jim Dance. I think maybe he's a cattle buyer. Anyway, he's looking for a friend that come here on that business.'

'Dance, eh?' The cowboy looked a bit uneasy. Then he forced a laugh. 'If he's a cattle buyer, I'm a ribbon salesman.'

'What gives you that idea, Buck?'

'I'll bet my poke,' Buck stated definitely, 'that he's one hell-roarin' gunfighter. Texas stuff, I'd call him. I've seen these easy-going, light-stepping hombres before, and they sure do pull their irons in a hurry when necessary. Nope, that hombre may be looking for cattle thieves—but I've got ten bucks he ain't looking for cattle.'

Jeff didn't offer to cover the bet.

Meanwhile, the Dancer had progressed down the main street until he reached a large, barn-like building in front of which burned several gasoline torches. The building was painted a lurid red. Across its front wall were big white letters that spelled the words: THE RED PHOENIX.

Men jostled each other at the wide, double-doored entrance as they went in or departed. From the interior came the strains of a tin-panny piano, and the sounds of glasses

37

clinking against bottle. The Dancer ascended the wide steps to the board platform that fronted the building and shoved his way inside.

The interior of the Red Phoenix was a bedlam of sound. Along the right-hand wall stretched a bar, behind which three perspiring bartenders toiled to assuage the thirst of the customers crowded three deep before them. On the left side of the room were the various games of chance—if *chance* it could be termed, in such a dive. Faro, roulette, the wheel, chuckaluck, blackjack and craps—plenty of ways for a man to lose his hard-earned cash. A squared space was roped off in the center of the room to be employed as a dance floor. Here a group of heavy-footed miners were revolving in the intricacies of a waltz, guided to some small extent by their short-skirted, heavily-rouged partners.

At the far end of the big room on a raised platform sat the orchestra consisting of an out-of-tune piano, a squeaky violin and a raspy cornet. Beyond the orchestra platform, a narrow flight of stairs led to a balcony that circled four sides of the room. Along the balcony were a number of curtained booths for those who desired to drink in privacy. Up here, also, was the office of Nick Grindall and Hutch Worden, the proprietors of the Red Phoenix.

At the bar, Dance got the attention of one of the bartenders. A glass and a bottle of cheap liquor were shoved before him. The

Dancer poured scarcely enough liquor to cover the bottom of his glass. As he was about to raise it to his lips, a man jostled his arm. Dancer turned suddenly, almost throwing the man off balance as their bodies collided.

'What in hell is the matter with you—' the man commenced angrily, then paused, mouth dropping open in dismay.

'Hallo, Taggert,' Dance said, smiling coldly.

Deuce Taggert shrank back. 'The Dancer!' he gasped hoarsely.

Dance nodded. 'You act surprised, Taggert.'

'Did—did you—follow me here?' Taggert stammered.

'Why should I? I didn't know where you were headed when you pulled out. Why should I follow you? Do you know of any good reason, Taggert?'

Taggert shook his head. The color was coming back to his face now. 'Well, no,' he said at last; 'only—only—well, I thought at first, maybe, you'd followed me to finish what was started—during that card game.'

The Dancer shook his head. 'I won that round,' he said quietly. 'So far as I'm concerned, your cheating is forgotten. Not that I hanker to play with you again, but I reckon you've learned your lesson. You're lucky I only scratched your arm a mite with my slug. I could have done better, Taggart. Just remember that, if you ever run counter to me again. After all, only a skunk deals crooked cards.'

'I reckon you're right, Dance.' Taggert hung his head as though ashamed. 'I shouldn't have done that, only—only I was hard-pressed for ready cash . . . You aiming to stay in Carabina a spell?'

'I haven't decided yet.'

'Well, it's a pretty good town—'

'—for a marked-card expert, eh?'

'I didn't say that, Dance . . . Let's have a drink.'

'No, thanks. I just had one. It was pretty terrible liquor.'

Taggert squeezed in beside him and ordered a slug of whisky. He downed the liquor then asked, 'Was Dobe Liston pretty sore at me for running those marked cards into the game?'

'I don't reckon,' Dance said flatly. 'There's no use of you lying, Taggert, or trying to bluff me. Liston was in on that game as deep as you—'

'Honest to Gawd, Dance, that's not so—'

'Don't lie, I told you,' Dance cut in coldly. 'Liston was hand-in-glove with you. He tried to gun me last night and again this morning. He made a third try when I stepped off the train for a short spell, on my way here.'

'No! I can't believe it—'

'Don't lie, I said.'

'Well—well, what happened? Did you finish him?'

40

The Dancer asked directly, 'What would you have done in my shoes, Taggert?'

'We-ell, I don't know—'

'I'll tell you then. You'll' find Liston's body among the sandhills about eight miles east of Floresburg—'

'My Gawd!'

'He was a friend of yours, Taggert. Prove your friendship by seeing he gets a decent burial. And just remember, he pushed me once too often. And something else, Taggert—I'm not craving to talk to you, about my business or anything else. The less I see of you, the better I like it. Is that plain?'

'Plain as hell,' Taggert snapped. 'I was willing to be friends but—'

'I couldn't be friends with a sidewinder—'

'You're going to wish you had been,' Taggert rasped. 'Wait and see if you don't.'

He whirled angrily away and was soon lost in the crowd. Dance glanced around. The noise of the orchestra and talk of customers had completely drowned out his conversation with Taggert. He wondered what Taggert's next move would be.

'I've got a hunch,' Dance mused, 'that there's bigger game waiting for my guns than Deuce Taggert. Something should break right soon.'

At that moment, his gaze caught Taggert ascending the stairs to the balcony. Dance watched the man until he reached the top. On the balcony, Taggert made his way around the side wall, stopped at a door, knocked, then entered. The door closed quickly behind him.

Dance ran his eyes along the balcony, past the line of curtained booths to the door where Taggert had disappeared.

'I'm betting that's Grindall's office,' Dance speculated.

His eyes were still on the door when it was abruptly flung open again. A girl emerged, slamming the door angrily behind her. She appeared considerably upset about something, judging from her determined walk and tilted chin. Dance watched her until she reached the top of the flight of stairs. As she descended, the illumination from the oil lamps, suspended above the floor of the honkytonk, threw her features into bold relief.

Dance frowned. This was no common dancehall girl. He wondered what her connection was with such a place as the Red Phoenix. She was tall and slim, blonde of hair, though her skin was tanned healthily with cow country color. Dance could never remember afterward what the girl wore that night. Something light and very feminine. That was all he could recollect afterward. The details escaped him.

A drunken miner sighted the girl. With a yell of triumph he started toward her. Dance started to move. He reached the girl just as the miner was asking her to dance. The girl refused. The miner's face darkened, then he said something else.

Smack! The girl's open palm descended with no little force on the miner's unshaven features. He staggered back, hat falling to the floor, then righted himself and started to swear.

And that was as far as he got when Dance's hand fell on his shoulder. 'That's enough, mister,' Dance said quietly. 'You'd better go some place and sleep off your liquor.'

The miner hiccoughed and stared, bleary-eyed, at Dance. 'What you say?' he growled.

'The lady doesn't want your company, hombre.'

'What's it to you, cowboy?'

Dance said swiftly to the girl, 'You'd better get out of here as soon as you can, miss. I'll keep this fellow busy—'

'I'll stay as long as you do,' she flashed. 'I'm not afraid of such scum—'

The Dancer was still trying to persuade the girl to depart when the miner known as Zach started to push in between them. 'You—you—' He stated belligerently, 'come here lookin' fer trouble. Well, I aims to satisfy yore cravin'. Now you'll get it!'

He started a slow, ponderous swing at Dance's head, which Dance had no trouble avoiding. The punch fell short, nearly carrying the drunken miner off balance.

Then the Dancer got into action; he came

stepping in, poised lightly on the balls of his feet. He hit the miner once, twice, three times. Blood spurted from the man's nose and mouth. He started to fall, but a comrade held him erect.

He swayed, vacant-eyed, a moment, trying to focus his gaze on the Dancer. Again Dance came stepping lightly in, and again his fists beat a rapid tattoo on the miner's face.

A howl went up from the crowd. Some jeered, a few laughed at the miner's clumsy attempts to defend himself. For the most part, though, the crowd was angry at Dance. The miner's arms were threshing about like flails, trying to find Dance's face. Dance's blows didn't travel far, but they possessed the lightning power of a panther's paw.

Abruptly, the miner crashed to the floor at the feet of his comrades! For a moment he lay still, then he spat out several broken teeth and climbed to his feet.

Dance held himself ready. 'Got enough?' he queried softly.

The miner swore at him, reached to the butt of a gun tucked inside his trousers' waist-band. 'Damn you!' he raged. 'I'll show you if I got enough!'

CHAPTER FIVE

The Dancer's left hand swept the girl behind him. His right swooped, lightning-like, to his hip. His gun was out, covering the miner before that drunken sot could jerk his own gun muzzle clear.

'Stick 'em high!' Dance snapped grimly. 'Don't pull it, fellow!'

His left gun was out now. The crowd began to back away. Most of them jerked their arms high in the air, following the suddenly frightened movement of the miner.

The Dancer spoke over his shoulder to the girl. 'Head for the entrance. We've got to get out of this, *pronto!*'

Slowly, they made their way to the bar, and then along the bar toward the wide doorway. The crowd moved reluctantly to allow them to pass. At the back of the room, several men voiced threats, or called advice to their comrades near Dance and the girl. Suddenly the girl gave a sharp cry of fear. The Dancer swung half-around, not daring to remove his eyes from the crowd. 'The—the balcony!' the girl gasped. 'That man up there—'

For a brief moment Dance glanced toward the balcony. Deuce Taggert was just emerging from Grindall's office doorway, a Winchester rifle clutched in his hands.

Taggert raised the rifle. Dance's left gun jerked up, belched a mushroom of smoke and orange flame. The Winchester cracked sharply, fire running from the barrel, but the bullet missed its mark, ripping viciously into the bar at Dance's rear. Dance's first shot had spoiled Deuce Taggert's aim.

Somewhere in the room, one of the dancehall girls screamed. Again Dance thumbed a swift shot toward the balcony.

Deuce Taggert stiffened, a look of surprise on his face. The rifle slipped from his fingers. Quite suddenly he staggered across the balcony railing, lost his balance and pitched to the floor below.

There came a wild rush to avoid the falling body. Again the dancehall girl screamed. It made the crowd panicky. There came a sudden rush of footsteps as the occupants of the Red Phoenix stampeded in a mad rush to gain the outer air.

Men and girls jammed the doorway, fighting to get out. Several of the dancehall girls were screaming now. Regardless of the situation or the place, Dance didn't want to see innocent people hurt. He was thinking fast, now.

'Hold it!' his voice rang through the big room. 'I'll be pouring lead if you don't stop!'

His words brought the crowd to its senses. It calmed down. Arms again shot into the air. Many of the less courageous near the entrance slipped outside. Slowly, the rest straggled back

46

into the center of the room.

On the balcony above, a big, dark-complexioned, bulky-shouldered man had appeared, and stood glowering down on those below.

'What's wrong down there?' he demanded harshly. 'Who done that shootin'?'

'That's Nick Grindall,' whispered the girl at Dance's shoulder.

Dance looked steadily at Grindall, taking in his heavy features, bushy eyebrows and thick jowls.

'I shot Taggert,' Dance replied grimly. 'He was throwing down on me, when I fired. It was self-defense. How does it happen, Grindall, you let him have that gun? He got it in your office.'

'Taggert works for me,' Grindall spat back. 'He was protecting my property. Who are you?'

'The name is Dance,' came the cold answer. 'Not that it makes any difference. I'll be leaving in a minute.' The Dancer felt certain Taggert had told Grindall of his arrival.

'Like hell you'll leave here,' Grindall roared angrily. 'You can't kill a man in the Red Phoenix and get away with it.' He snapped out orders to the crowd below. 'Some of you hombres wake up. Are you going to let one man shove his guns down your throat? Where's your nerve? Are you going to let Dance kill Deuce Taggert and then live to

47

boast of it? If you do, you're yellow. Show some life, unless you're a bunch of sheep!'

An angry muttering ran through the crowd. Again, Dance's guns came up, the barrels swinging in wide arcs that covered every person in the room. 'I'll be slinging lead at the first move,' he vowed grimly. 'Keep your hands away from your guns, every man jack of you. You, too, Grindall. I'd just as soon bore you— sooner, in fact, than any man in the room.'

A curse broke from Grindall, but he moved back from the balcony railing. Again, Dance and the girl started toward the doorway. As they neared the entrance, he swung around to back out, thus keeping his eyes on the crowd. The girl backed slowly at his side, her eyes and senses as alert as his own.

Even the bartenders behind the long mahogany counter had their arms in the air, now. There seemed certain death in Dance's stern features for the first man to make a hostile move. No one wanted to take a chance of starting anything. The Dancer had the roomful of men completely cowered, no doubt of that.

He was within a foot of the exit when what he'd been fearing most took place. He hadn't dared to look over his shoulder, for fear someone might draw and fire. And then, just as he and the girl were about to step into the open air, Dance felt something round and cold and hard, jabbed against his spine, and a hard voice gave orders.

'Put those guns away, hombre. It's sure death if you don't move fast!'

There wasn't anything uncertain about that voice. It meant business. The Dancer knew he couldn't take risks at this stage of the game. When he acted, he'd have to act with considerable speed and dispatch.

He shrugged his shoulders in careless surrender. 'You win, hombre,' he said tonelessly, dropping his guns at his sides, then lifting them as though to slide the weapons back into holsters.

He felt the gun barrel removed from the small of his back. At the same moment the girl at his side said something he didn't catch. Dance was moving too fast for words now. Just as his gun barrels touched holsters, he spun swiftly about, snapping them waist high again!

There came a startled gasp of surprise from the man who had, but an instant before, had the Dancer covered.

Dance laughed softly. Noticing a star of office on the man's vest, he said quietly, 'It looks like a deadlock, sheriff. You've got me covered, but you're in the same fix yourself.'

The girl was speaking again. 'Mr. Dance! It's all right. Put down your guns. This is Sheriff Purdy. Sheriff, don't shoot! This man is a friend. He helped me—'

'Good Lord! Polly! What you doing here?'

The girl had been noticed by the sheriff for

49

the first time. His surprised gaze swept back to Dance, and his face crimsoned as he thought of how Dance had fooled him.

Dance took the sheriff in at a glance and saw a tall spare man in black clothing and with sweeping yellow moustaches, probably fifty years of age. Dance lowered his guns, saying, 'Sheriff, so long as she vouches for you'—and he jerked his head toward the girl—'I'll take a chance on your guns.'

Again he spun around to cover the crowd, his back to the peace officer. It had all happened so quickly that the slow-witted crowd hadn't thought to get a gun into action while Dance was occupied with the sheriff. Or perhaps the arrival of the sheriff had rendered further aid in taking the courage out of the already cowed men gathered inside the Red Phoenix.

The girl was explaining to the sheriff just what had happened, when Nick Grindall broke in from the balcony, 'Sheriff Purdy, I demand that you arrest that man. He's either killed, or badly injured, one of my trusted employees, Deuce Taggert.'

The sheriff chuckled dryly and spoke to Dance. 'You put yore guns away, mister. Nobody won't be startin' anythin' now. You wait with Polly while I drift in and see what sort of a job you made on Taggert. I'll hear yore story in a few minutes.'

'Right-o.' Dance smiled, holstering his guns.

50

He rejoined the girl while the sheriff crossed the floor to kneel at Taggert's side. Meanwhile, the others in the Red Phoenix sauntered uneasily up to the bar for drinks, or stood watching the sheriff in nervous silence.

By the time the sheriff had returned, Dance had learned the girl's name was Polly Loomis. He refused to listen to any word of thanks from the girl, for the part he had played in protecting her from the drunken miner—who, incidentally, had disappeared.

'We're all square, Miss Loomis,' Dance said. 'If you hadn't warned me when Taggert was lifting that Winchester, I reckon I'd not be alive this minute. Seems like the obligations are—'

At that moment the sheriff returned. He nodded grimly to Dance. 'You made a complete job of it, mister. I've given order to have Taggert's body removed. I'd like to hear, now, just what happened. First, what's yore name?'

'Dance—Jim Dance.'

Sam Purdy's eyes widened. 'Cripes. No wonder you got the drop on me, when I had you covered. I don't feel so 'shamed as I did. I've heard of *you*. You used to be—'

'Let's not go into details, sheriff,' Dance suggested with a smile.

Dance and Sheriff Purdy escorted Polly to the street, disregarding the angry looks that followed them through the door.

51

'I've got to get all of this story,' Purdy was saying, when they reached the sidewalk. 'What say you two come down to my office. Polly, how come you were in the Red Phoenix? That ain't any place for a girl like you.'

Polly Loomis commenced to explain as the three of them walked along the street. 'My father—that is, Nick Grindall sent for me. You know how things have been going, sheriff. Grindall said if I'd come to see him, he'd get everything squared away to my satisfaction. On Dick's account I went there and—'

'Well'—Purdy snorted indignantly—'if Grindall ain't the poorest excuse for a father I ever see, asking his daughter to step into that purgatory of crooks and cutthroats!'

Nick Grindall, Polly Loomis's father!

The Dancer could scarcely believe his ears. The girl evidently realized what was passing through Dance's mind, for she turned to him, and said, 'Grindall isn't my real father, Mr. Dance. He's just my stepfather.'

Dance felt relieved.

The sheriff said, 'Jim and I will walk along to Ma Morley's with you, Polly. There's sort of a rough crowd on the streets, these nights.'

'I'll be glad of the company,' the girl said.

The three stepped out to the street.

As they headed along the sidewalk, jostled on all sides by moving men, Sheriff Purdy said, 'By the way, Polly, what were Nick Grindall's plans for you? You didn't mention that.'

The girl hesitated, then, 'He offered to marry me, and then make a will leaving the outfit to me—'

The sheriff swore suddenly, excused himself, then changed the subject. The girl didn't reopen it.

Ten minutes later, Dance and Purdy had left Polly at her boardinghouse, on one of the cross streets, and were again back on the main thoroughfare. The sheriff was strangely quiet, except for a muttered, indignant oath, now and then.

'I'll try to tell you about Polly,' he said after a while.

'I'm listening.'

'To begin with,' Purdy commenced, 'Mrs. Loomis—that is, Polly's mother, was a widow when she first hit this range, back about eight years ago. Her husband had died up in Montana, some place where the Loomis family ran a cow outfit. Mrs. Loomis had sold her holdin's and come to this country, bringing Polly and young Dick—Dick is Polly's brother, who's about a year or so younger than Polly.'

The sheriff paused to stuff tobacco into an old briar pipe. Dance rolled and lighted a cigarette. The sheriff puffed reminiscently and continued, 'But Mrs. Loomis had cowraisin' in her blood. To cut a long story short, she bought the Bow-Knot outfit, which lays twelve miles west of Carabina. At that time, the Bow-Knot had a pretty good crew, rodded by Nick

Grindall who was foreman.'

'Grindall must have changed a heap since those days.'

'He shore did.' Purdy frowned. 'We used to think Grindall was a pretty good hombre, but we'd never seen him in his true light, I reckon. Anyway, running a cow ranch was a pretty big job for Mrs. Loomis. She'd sent Dick and Polly away to school in another state. Dick worked when he was home, durin' vacations, but, all in all, the Bow-Knot was too big a problem for Mrs. Loomis to handle alone.'

'And so,' Dance put in, 'she married Nick Grindall.'

Purdy nodded. 'Grindall must have pulled the wool over her eyes in fine shape. But you know how some widows are. Anyway, Mrs. Loomis thought a heap of Grindall at first, but he turned out to be such a dirty dog that he run her into an early grave. You see, most folks blame Grindall's actions for Mrs. Loomis' death—or, by this time, Mrs. Grindall's death, to be correct. Grindall had a hand in drawing up her will, and fixed things so Polly and Dick can't get control of the Bow-Knot, unless Grindall dies. At the same time, if Polly and Dick were to pass out sudden, Grindall would inherit their interests.'

The Dancer whistled softly. 'Looks like Polly and Dick were sitting on the edge of a cliff with an avalanche bearing down at their rear. Dam'd if I see how their mother ever come to agree to such a will.'

'Ain't I told you Grindall pulled the wool over her eyes? In spite of his crooked ways, she sort of trusted him to the last. She couldn't believe the change that had come over him. It's two years since she died. From that minute on, Grindall has done everything he can to get Polly and Dick out of the country, so he'll have things his own way.'

'What's Grindall been doing to them?'

'Makin' life tough for both those kids. He made Polly work around the outfit, like she was a hired woman and refused to give her a penny. Dick, the same way. Grindall kept that boy ridin' herd for three days once without letting him have a wink of sleep or a bite to eat. On Polly's account and because of his mother's memory, Dick never did bring things to an open break. He just rolled his blankets and pulled out of the outfit. He went away for a time. He's back, though, now, riding for the Rafter-N spread. He hates Grindall like poison.'

'I should think,' Dance said softly, 'that Polly and Dick could take matters into court and—'

'Not a bit of use,' Purdy interrupted. 'Grindall has got control of the ranch until he dies. It's all in black and white. 'Course, he promised Polly's mother he'd always look after the two young 'uns, but with a skunk like Grindall a promise doesn't mean anything.'

'I suppose not.'

'A week ago Polly, not being able to put up with Grindall and his ways any longer, moved into town. She told me she was plumb sick of cooking and washing dishes for the crew Grindall has with him now.'

The Dancer's eyes were hot. 'It's a crime,' he snapped.

The sheriff nodded, spat angrily and went on, 'Dick hasn't heard about that, yet. He hasn't been to town and he never goes near the Bow-Knot any more. I'm looking for hell to break loose when the boy does hear the news. The boy's hot-tempered and prone to jump into action without thinking. Then, tonight, you heard Polly say that Grindall had offered to square matters by offering to marry her. The sneaking, dirty buzzard. Can you imagine a clean, decent girl like Polly givin' herself in marriage to a skunk like Grindall! It fair makes my blood boil.'

The Dancer's face was hard. He nodded slowly, thinking. He didn't say anything.

'And when Dick hears about that offer of marriage,' Purdy growled, 'I'm afraid I'm going to have my hands full to prevent him from killing Grindall—or getting himself murdered.'

'Well,' Dance speculated quietly, 'if Dick did kill Grindall, it would at least give him and Polly what rightfully should be theirs.'

'The boy could never do it,' Purdy said.

'Grindall fast with his hardware?'

'One of the best. Probably there ain't a man in town can match him—except maybe Hutch Worden. Worden has a rep for being unbeatable. When I say there ain't a man in town can beat them two, Jim, I wasn't taking you into consideration. Probably either of 'em would be duck soup for you.'

The Dancer looked troubled. 'I don't know, Sam. I had a tough time once, beating Worden to the shot. I might not be so lucky next time. Maybe he's improved since then. Well, we'll see.'

'See what?' the sheriff demanded.

'We'll see what we see.' Dance smiled tiredly. He rose, stretched his arms and yawned. 'I'm going to drift along to the hotel and get some shut-eye. I'm not ready yet, Sam, to state what brings me here, but when the right time comes I may have to ask your help.'

'I'll be waiting for you to tell—and so will Chuck Osborn.'

'That's fine, Sam . . . Well, good-night.'

'Good-night, Jim.'

Dance stepped out to the street and thoughtfully made his way to the hotel. Now, in addition to the problem he'd come to Carabina to settle, he found himself wanting to take on Polly Loomis' troubles and dispose of them. The girl's eyes and her smile had done something to the Dancer's heart that night. He found himself wanting to keep that smile on

57

the girl's face for always, and it was of Polly Loomis he was thinking as he dropped off to sleep that night.

CHAPTER SIX

Hutch Worden was plainly worried when he burst into his office in the Red Phoenix. Below, in the honkytonk, business had fallen off to a considerable degree. Deuce Taggert's death had thrown a damper on the usual riotous proceedings. Only a few dancers revolved on the dance floor. Most of the games were idle. A large number of the customers had departed, and the few who remained at the bar weren't drinking to any extent.

'What in hell's happened to business?' Worden demanded, slamming the office door at his back and facing Nick Grindall, who was slouched morosely in an easy-chair in one corner.

Grindall glanced up. 'Looks like it has gone haywire,' he growled sullenly. 'Some feller by the name of Dance come in here and a little time after Deuce Taggert had told me this Dance was plumb poisonous, dam'd if Taggert don't step out on the balcony with a Winchester in his hand and prove his statement—much to Taggert's sorrow, if he

58

had any time to be sorry after Dance's slugs ripped home. All this took the steam out of the crowd. Sam Purdy came here. I tried to make him arrest Dance, but—'

'Yeah, I know most of the story,' Worden interrupted. 'Nick, this is a damn' bad break for us. I don't like it.'

'What do you mean?'

'The Dancer.'

'What about him? Who is he?'

Worden found a chair and sat down. He ripped out a sudden oath. 'Jim Dance—the Dancer—is the man who put me behind bars. One time he was a captain in the Texas Rangers. I tangled with him and I didn't do so well. I had hard luck. Two years ago he resigned from the Rangers. No one ever discovered why, to my knowledge.'

Grindall looked worried. 'Do you think he's on our trail?'

'I can't figure how he could be. At the same time, we can't afford to take chances. If he's trailing anybody, though, and I have a hunch he is, it might be some of our crowd. I don't like it. What did Taggert say about him?'

'Not much, but enough to show he's poison. He'd caught Taggert cheating in a poker game and winged him. Taggert lit out for here. A few hours later, Dance showed up—'

'Had he trailed Taggert here?'

'Taggert didn't think so. At the same time, he couldn't account for Dance getting here so

59

soon—'

Grindall broke off as the office door opened to admit a man of slight figure, with stooping shoulders and scraggly white hair. No cow country product, this individual. His watery blue eyes were continually shifting and his manner was nervous. He entered quietly and closed the door behind him. His name was Tracy Chapman and while he shared in the ill-gotten gains of Worden and Grindall, he had no holdings in the Red Phoenix.

As Chapman found a chair and sat down, Worden said to him, 'Tracy, do you remember when we were in the pen, together, I told you about a feller called the Dancer?'

Chapman nodded. 'I'm not likely to forget. You spent most of your sentence cursing him.'

'I'll curse him as long as I live,' Worden said bitterly. His manner abruptly quieted. 'The Dancer is in Carabina, Tracy.'

Chapman's face paled. 'Is he the same man who killed Taggert tonight?'

'The same.'

'Judas! Is he after us?'

'I don't think so, but we can't take any chances. He's a fox, that hombre, and he's got a pair of guns to back up his thinking qualities. I'd feel more comfortable if he wasn't here in town.'

'What's the answer?' Chapman wanted to know.

Worden said hard-voiced, 'The Dancer has

60

got to be put out of the way.'

Chapman licked at his suddenly dry lips. 'That ain't my work,' he said nervously. 'I do my part, but I'm no murderer. I can't shoot a man. That's up to you and Nick. You two take care of the Dancer and I'll run my end of the business.'

'Oh, hell,' Grindall growled. 'There's no use of all this palaverin'. What's the answer, Hutch, do you plug Dance, or do I?'

Worden shook his head. 'That's just the rub, Nick. You're not fast enough to get him—'

'T'hell I ain't—'

'I'm telling you, Nick. I'm faster'n you, but Dance is—'

'You afraid of him?'

Worden flushed. 'Not by a damn sight. But I don't see any use of taking unnecessary chances. I don't want to cross guns with him, unless absolutely necessary.'

Chapman said again, 'Well, what's the answer?'

'I was thinking it over on the way here,' Worden said slowly, 'and I figure Blade Otornik is the man for our money.'

'Huh!' Grindall looked up in surprise. 'You mean that knife toter who's always boasting how good he is?'

'The same.' Worden nodded. 'In spite of Blade Otornik's boasting, he *is* good. He's got a right to boast. I've known him quite a spell now. I've seen him in action. He's deadly with a knife. Down in Mexico he has the rep of being the fastest knife in the Southwest. You have to be good to get that kind of a rep down there—'

'He's no Mexican,' Grindall put in.

'I didn't say he was. Gawd knows what Blade is—he seems to be a mixture of everything under the sun. But he's neat with a knife—like a streak of lightning. There's no stopping him, once he gets started.'

'But how do you figure—'

'Here's the way I dope it out,' Worden said. 'We can't take any chances on the Dancer hanging around here. I've got a score to settle with him, anyway. Nick, you and I might out-shoot him, and I think we could, but we'd run the risk of getting plugged ourselves. Why not let Blade Otornik do the job? He'll take it on for a hundred dollars—'dobe dollars—and be glad to get the money.'

'I'm agreeable.' Grindall nodded, then added dubiously, 'But I don't see how you expect to work the Dancer in a position for Blade Otornik to knife him. I doubt if Blade could slip up behind him and—'

'You leave this to me.' Worden grinned nastily. 'I know the Dancer. Once he's committed to a fight, he won't back out. He's good with guns, but is probably a fool with a knife in his hand. We'll have Blade challenge him. Knowing the Dancer like I do, I know he won't back out even when he finds out knives, instead of guns, are to be used. He'd go through with it, even if Death was staring him in the face.'

Tracy Chapman said, 'Blade Otornik is downstairs now. Want me to get him up here?'

'That's a good idea.' Worden nodded.

The door closed on Chapman.

Grindall said, 'Where are you figuring to hold this duel, Hutch?'

'Right in the Red Phoenix.' Worden chuckled. 'Right in plain view of everybody present, so the sheriff won't be able to arrest us on a murder charge.'

'How do you plan to get the Dancer over here?'

'That won't be any trouble. I know his methods. He'll likely drop in tomorrow, just to look around. He's looking for somebody, all right, and he won't pass up the Red Phoenix in his search.'

'It might work at that,' Grindall muttered.

'Certainly it will work.' Worden grinned triumphantly. 'You'll see that I know what I'm talking about.'

The office door opened and Chapman returned, followed by a tall, powerfully built man in blue corduroys, a scarlet shirt and a fawn colored sombrero. Spurs jangled musically on his high-heeled boots. His eyes had a certain Oriental slant to them, but it was plain to be seen from the rest of his evil features that he was a mixture of the worst to be found in a dozen different races.

'Blade,' Worden opened the conversation, 'I've got a job for your knife.'

Otornik's eyes brightened. 'Good,' he spoke in a thick, guttural voice 'I need the money. Your damn faro dealer took my last red cent. But my knife is ready any time. The job is as good as finished. You won't find a faster blade in the whole Southwest than Otornik. There ain't a man can face me with steel—'

'All right, all right, Otornik,' Grindall growled. 'Keep your trap shut a few minutes. We've heard all that before. Just sit down and listen close to what Hutch is going to say. This is damn important.'

*   *   *

It was mid-morning of the following day, when Dance encountered Deputy Chuck Osborn on the main street of Carabina.

Osborn greeted him in mournful accents, 'Mornin', Dancer.'

'Hullo, Chuck,' Dance smiled, 'you just heading to get a cup of tea?'

Osborn shook his head. 'I can't even take tea, this mornin',' he said sadly. 'My stomach won't hold a thing. I'm plumb upset. This town is too quiet this mornin'. I don't like it.'

'It's quiet every morning, isn't it? It should be with the miners back at work and the drunks sleeping off their bats.'

'This mornin' seems different. I'm just a mess of jumpin' nerves.' The deputy shook his head worriedly. 'I'm all shot to pieces. This town has me scared. I'm going to resign. I was just heading for the general store to see if they had any headache powders for a sick headache.'

'Who's got the headache?' Dance grinned. 'Some prisoner that tried to get tough with you in his cell this morning?'

Osborn looked reproachfully at Dance. 'I can see you've been talkin' to Sam Purdy. Now, the news will be all over town. I always feel ashamed of myself when I lose my temper that way, but it made me sort of peeved for a second, when that prisoner broke the platter of breakfast I'd brought him, over my head.'

'I'd say he used damn bad judgment,' Dance chuckled.

'Anyway, the headache powder is for me, you can understand.'

'How about a shot of bourbon for that headache?'

Osborn brightened a trifle. 'There! I never thought of bourbon, but I've heard it was good for headaches. I understand the Cowman's Rest Hotel keeps a good grade of bourbon in the bar.'

'We'll inspect it . . . You're not in a hurry, are you? I'd like to drop into the Red Phoenix and look around a mite, on our way to the Cowman's Rest.'

65

'The liquor in the Red Phoenix is rot-gut,' Osborn warned.

'I'm not surprised. But I'd just like to drop in a few minutes and see who hangs out there.'

'That ain't necessary. I can tell you right now that the place is infected with skunks. But come on. We can wash up, afterward.'

The Red Phoenix was considerably quieter than it had been on Dance's visit of the evening before. There were only a few customers at the bar. The gaming tables were sheathed in oilcloth covers. The instruments on the orchestra platform were also covered. None of the girls was in sight.

Dance noticed Blade Otornik at the far end of the bar as he and Osborn entered. Osborn nudged Dance's arm. 'That's Blade Otornik,' the deputy said. 'I understand he's bad, but he hasn't done anything in Carabina I could take him up on.'

They moved on, to the bar. A bartender took their orders. Dance sent a twenty-dollar gold piece ringing down the mahogany counter and poured a modest drink. Osborn was also conservative.

The barkeep made change, giving Dance three five-dollar bills, two ones and some silver.

Dance asked, 'This all the silver you have?'

'Pretty short this morning.' The barkeep nodded. 'Don't you like bills?'

'I prefer silver,' Dance said. 'However, if

you haven't got it, you haven't, that's all.'

He slid the silver the bartender had given him, together with the one-dollar bills, in a side pocket. The three five-dollar bills he placed inside his vest. Finishing his drink he commenced to roll a cigarette.

Tracy Chapman, who had been talking to Otornik, at the end of the bar, now left and went up on the balcony to enter Grindall's and Worden's office.

In a short time, Grindall and Worden, accompanied by Chapman, appeared on the balcony and descended the stairs to take places at the bar.

Worden nodded briefly to Dance. Grindall scowled. Dance laughed softly. He had a feeling that all wasn't as it should have been, that something was due to happen. At the same time, he failed to analyse his feelings, and finally decided he was growing uneasy over nothing. Finally, he turned to Chuck Osborn, saying, 'If you're ready, I am. Let's move along.'

Osborn nodded. 'My headache is getting worse. It always does in this joint.'

The two started toward the door, when Blade Otornik swung around, advanced toward them, then stopped within a few feet of Dance. Dance stopped.

Otornik said, 'Do you always have to have silver when the bartender makes change, feller?'

'Not necessarily,' Dance returned coolly. He wondered what was afoot. Something warned him to move carefully.

'Huh,' Otornik sneered, 'just trying to make yourself sound important so folks would notice you, eh? You want everybody to see the Dancer. Just because you've won a few gunfights don't get the idea you're a great man. Dancer hell!'

'Oh, go to blazes.' Dance laughed, concluding Otornik must have been drinking too much. He started to turn away.

Otornik caught at his arm. 'Just a minute, hombre. I'm Blade Otornik, the best damn knife man in the Southwest. I'm as good as you, any day. Better, in fact. Now, I've got something to say to you.'

'Maybe I'm not interested,' Dance replied quietly. 'To tell the truth, I know I'm not.'

'Hell's bells!' Otornik snarled. 'You can't talk to me that way. I won't take it. Must be you're looking for a fight.'

Chuck Osborn broke in, 'What's the idea, Otornik?' Then to his companion, 'Careful, Dance. This doesn't look good.' He swung back to the knife man. 'You, Otornik, keep a civil tongue in your head or I'll stick you in a cell—'

'Let me handle this, Chuck,' Dance cut in. He turned back to Otornik, saying, 'So you're Blade Otornik, eh? I heard of a Blade Otornik being run out of Laredo once for throwing

68

knives at sheep. Personally, I always figured him for a cheap, no-good coyote who didn't have the nerve to pack a gun.'

Dance added other things that made Otornik's face turn crimson with rage.

Finally, the knife man found his tongue. 'You've said too much, hombre,' he snarled. 'You've got to fight me, if you got the nerve. Otherwise, I'll run you out of town at the end of one of my blades. Will you fight, or won't you?'

'Sure, I'll fight,' Dance snapped. 'Go get a gun.'

Otornik shook his head. 'I'm no gunman. We'll fight with knives. If you refuse you're a yellow-bellied dog with the nerve of a stink bird. Quick, make up your mind. Are you going to fight, or turn tail like all your breed?'

The Dancer's face was a granite-like mask. 'Bring on your knives,' he said coldly. 'I've stuck pigs before. Go get 'em.'

Triumphantly, Otornik turned away. 'It won't take but a minute, Dancer,' he sneered over one shoulder.

Chuck Osborn groaned. 'Oh, hell, Dancer, you're in for it now. Otornik's a wizard with a knife. You're meeting him at his own game. Come on, call it off, and we'll get out of here.'

Worden, Grindall, Chapman and other men at the bar were laughing openly. Dance saw he'd been trapped. He realized he was in a jam. His face turned a shade whiter as he shook his head. 'No, Chuck, I'll have to see this through, now. Sometimes, you have to meet a man at his own game to show him who's boss. It might be I'll get a lucky break. If I don't—well—well, there's no use talking of that.'

'Did you ever use a knife, any?' Osborn queried.

'None to speak of. I've never fought with one.'

Osborn said hopelessly, 'Cripes A'mighty.' He added, 'I'll tell you. I'll stop this fight by arresting Otornik.'

'Don't do that, Chuck. I can't back out now. It would make me a laughing stock—worse. I couldn't finish the job I've come here to do. I can see it all now. All this is Worden's trap. I *know* that, but I've got to go through with it. I've given my word.'

He turned and, accompanied by Osborn, came back to the center of the room.

CHAPTER SEVEN

'Worden,' Dance said slowly, as he and Osborn approached the bar, 'this is your work. Are you too yellow to shoot it out with me? Do you have to hire somebody to do your killing?'

'I can't see why you should crab to me,' Worden sneered. 'This ain't my doings. You

70

got yourself into a fight with Otornik, and now you're trying to hold me responsible.'

'It's in your place.'

'Just because you're in the Red Phoenix is no sign I'm back of this.' Worden laughed insolently. 'I didn't ask you to come in here. You got only yourself to blame. If I had my way you'd never have come in here. You ain't got any kick. Carabina's deputy sheriff is with you. He can stop the fight if he wants to. That's his job—not mine. I ain't the law in this town.'

'By Gawd,' Chuck broke in, 'I will stop it, too. Otornik, don't you—'

'Let be, Chuck,' Dance interrupted quietly. 'I'm not backing you. Don't stop this ruckus on my account. You just sort of stick around to see that I get a square deal.'

Reluctantly, Osborn fell silent. He looked worried, knowing as he did Otornik's reputation as a knife man.

Grindall laughed harshly. 'There ain't nothing to hold Dance here, if he wants to run. The door ain't locked.'

Otornik sneered. 'When I prick him with the point of my blade you'll see him run, plenty fast. No man has ever yet stood against Blade Otornik with a knife in his hand and lived to boast of that fact—'

'Oh, shucks,' Dance said wearily, 'cut out the talk and let's get this business over with.'

He wasn't missing the looks of triumph on

the faces of the other men in the big room. Including the two owners of the Red Phoenix, Chapman and Otornik, there were fifteen men in the place.

By this time, Otornik had drawn down to the end of the bar. Some of the others gathered about him watching him strip to the waist in preparation for the fight. Osborn and Dance moved off by themselves and stood near the center of the bar.

Dance commenced to remove his guns and belts, then slipped off his vest and rolled up his shirt sleeves. The guns and belts he handed to Chuck with the advice, 'Keep these handy. You may have to use 'em before we get out of here. Watch Grindall and Worden close. No telling what they might try. I'll be having my hands full with this bloodthirsty Otornik hombre.'

Grindall spoke to a man standing near him. The man walked to the big entrance-way and closed the double doors, then returned grinning slyly at Dance and Osborn. The deputy opened his mouth to voice a protest, but Dance stopped him.

'But I don't like this, Dancer,' Chuck persisted. 'We're shut off, complete. They're probably afraid Sam Purdy will arrive and put a stop to this—'

'Let it slide,' Dance laughed softly. 'I've been in worse jams and come out with a whole skin. You've still got the guns. If necessary we'll shoot our way out—'

'Providing you are—' Osborn stopped abruptly.

'Providing I'm alive,' Dance completed the deputy's thought. 'Well, if I'm not—shucks, it won't make a great deal of difference. They don't dare touch you. It's me they're after. If my luck holds I'll give this Otornik the trimming of his life—'

'Dammit, you can't do it, Dancer. You don't savvy cold steel like he does.'

'That,' the Dancer said grimly, 'is just my tough luck, then. But I can try, anyhow.'

The Dancer saw now that Otornik was standing in his bare feet. Dance slipped off his own high-heeled boots and stood in his socks. As a last thought he tossed his sombrero with his vest on the bar.

Otornik was approaching him now, two knives held in his right hand.

'You get the choice Dancer,' he sneered. 'I'll give you that much of a break. But there's no difference in the blades. The difference comes when we take 'em in our hands.'

Suspicious of a trick, the Dancer looked the knives over carefully before choosing the one he was to use. They had long, keen-edged blades. Both showed signs of recent sharpening. The Dancer wondered how long back this fight had been planned. The handles of the knives were similarly formed, though one was of wood and the other bone.

'Which is your personal weapon, Otornik?'

Dance asked.

The knife man indicated the bone-handled blade. 'But take the one you want. In the end it will all be the same.'

And then, to Otornik's extreme surprise, Dance laughed as though at some huge joke. 'I reckon,' Dance drawled, 'this wood-handled blade will do for my cockroach carving. I reckon the joke's on you Otornik. You had an idea I didn't know anything about knife fighting, didn't you? Well, you've got a big surprise coming.'

It was a magnificent bluff on Dance's part. A suspicious look flitted across Otornik's features. He looked quickly toward Grindall and Worden. They, too, had suddenly sobered. After all, Worden considered, what did he really know about Dance. Dance was an excellent shot. He might be equally good with a knife.

The Dancer laughed again, picked up the knife with the wooden handle and balanced it in his hand. Something in his confident, carefree air commenced to weaken Otornik's courage. He wondered if he, himself, had fallen into the trap laid for Dance.

'Come on, Otornik,' Dance jerked over one shoulder and starting toward the center of the floor, then added to Osborn, 'I'll be with you in a minute, Chuck, just as soon as I carve me a roast pig. I haven't forgotten that bourbon for your headache, but this won't take long.'

Osborn couldn't reply. A lump swelled in his throat. He alone realized that Dance was running a strong bluff in the hope of gaining a small advantage over the other man's skill.

Worden followed Dance with anxious eyes. Dance stood in the center of the big room, the knife resting lightly in his right hand. Otornik, mouth still open with surprise, tinged with a quick nameless fear, stood as before, his eyes glued on Dance. Otornik was commencing to get worried. In all of his previous victories, he had never yet seen an opponent who seemed so carelessly confident of winning.

'Get going, Blade,' Worden called irritably. 'You going to take all night to start?'

Dance drawled, 'Don't rush him, Worden. He's just figured it out that the longer he waits, the longer he'll live. Even you should understand that.'

Otornik flushed crimson. With a savage oath he rushed out to the dance floor where Dance awaited him, and came to a stop a scant two yards away. 'Damn your hide!' Otornik snarled. 'Just for that I'm going to finish you within one second flat and—'

'Save your breath,' Dance cut in. 'You'll need it.'

The fight commenced. Gripping their knives firmly, the two combatants circled warily about the floor, crouching on bent knees, bodies tense. Of the two Otornik appeared to be the heavier, though he moved

75

as lithely as did the Dancer.

'Something was said about finishing this fight in one second flat,' Chuck Osborn commented loudly. 'Time's up, Otornik. It looks like you'll lose.'

Otornik didn't reply. No one else spoke. A silence descended on the big room, broken only by the breathing of the duelists and the sounds of their light steps on the wooden flooring. Twice, Otornik came in and each time, as Dance raised his knife to meet the attack, Otornik retreated. But Dance knew he couldn't maintain the bluff much longer. However, by this time, Dance was getting the feel of the business; it was something like boxing, so far as footwork and feinting went.

Suddenly Chuck Osborn's voice sounded again. 'Go get him, Dancer. He's yore meat!'

An oath broke from Otornik's lips. He leaped in to attack. There came a lightning flash of bluish light as his knife described a swift arc in the air. The Dancer slipped easily to one side, hearing the hiss of the cold steel as it slashed past him. He smiled, whirling to meet Otornik's next thrust. His own knife flashed out in a wicked swing that missed its mark, but caused Otornik to increase his caution.

Again, Otornik rushed. This time, Dance parried the stroke with his own blade. There came a swift slithering of naked steel. The Dancer shifted suddenly, drove in his own blade. Again, he missed as his opponent slipped to one side.

The two men circled about, each seeking an opening. Dance commenced to feel more confident. He commenced to employ boxing tactics. By watching Otornik's eyes and feet, he could tell just when the man was about to attack. And he would act accordingly.

Otornik rushed again. Dance moved to avoid the thrust a moment too late. The keen blade ripped open one shirt sleeve, above the elbow.

The Dancer forced a smile. 'Nice work, feller. I didn't think you had it in you.' At the same instant he lashed out with his own blade. Otornik tried to avoid the stroke, but underestimated Dance's speed. Like magic, a thin streak of scarlet appeared on the man's forearm.

'Yippee!' Chuck Osborn howled. 'First blood for Dance!'

Worden's angry curse cut in on the deputy's words. Others, now, commenced calling encouragement to Otornik.

Infuriated by the scratch on his arm, Otornik came plunging in, his knife working with lightning-like rapidity. Dance was hard-pressed to withstand the furious assault. Steel rang and quivered against steel. Otornik commenced to breathe heavily.

Suddenly, Dance shot in a straight stroke. In the nick of time, Otornik caught the blow on his own blade and turned it aside. Before Dance could recover, Otornik's steel had touched his side, slashing through his shirt. Dance was off balance now. He felt something warm against his flesh and knew that Otornik had drawn blood.

'Ha!' Otornik taunted. 'Now you'll see!'

Worden and his cohorts were calling exultant advice now. Otornik came in, swift as a striking panther in his strokes. Dance retreated back . . . back . . . then, swiftly sidestepped. Somehow, he fought off the attack by dodging, parrying, moving out of reach. For the next few moments, Dance didn't try any strokes of his own. He was too occupied in keeping his own body from harm to do any attacking.

Sweat broke out on his forehead, trickled down into his eyes. Within his shirt was that sticky warm feeling. Before his eyes was always Otornik's cruelly slashing blade and the man's hate-contorted face, as he bore in and in.

Around and around the two men circled, Dance ever giving ground before the attack. Their feet padded more swiftly on the floor; their breaths were coming in gasps now.

Even Otornik was astonished at the manner in which Dance had avoided his best strokes. The knife man was commencing to tire too. Dance's better condition was beginning to count now.

Abruptly, to gain his wind, Otornik paused.

Dance came in like a flash. Otornik broke ground. Dance's blade shot out in a vicious underhand stroke intended for Otornik's middle. Otornik moved like a streak of white lightning, catching Dance's blade, waist-high, on his own knife.

For a moment, neither man moved, as each exerted every ounce of strength to force back the arm of the other. The two knives appeared to be welded, blade to blade as each strained against the other.

Then, slowly and surely, Dance's steel-like muscles began to prevail. Back . . . slowly back . . . Otornik moved . . .

Abruptly, with a sobbing breathless curse, Otornik leaped out of reach, shifted, plunged back into the fray. His sudden attack was furious, bewildering. Dance was forced to retreat the length of the dance hall, before Otornik began to weaken.

Finally, the knife man paused. Dance charged in, sidestepped a vicious upthrust of Otornik's blade and drove in one of his own. Again, Otornik parried the stroke. Dance slipped to one side, drove in a straight thrust for the lower ribs!

Otornik stopped it just in time, catching Dance's blade on his own steel. The knives locked. Sweat poured into their eyes as Dance braced his arm against Otornik's. The men pressed closer and closer, each refusing to give an inch.

The others in the big room were silent now, straining to watch every move of the duelists. Not a word was spoken. Heard only was the long-tortured breathing of the two fighters, as they strained against each other, neither daring to lower his knife.

Suddenly, Dance threw caution to the winds. He flung himself sidewise, releasing his weapon. Too late, Otornik realized he had been outwitted. He tried to save himself, but was thrown off balance and caught in an awkward position.

Dance feinted for Otornik's face, then, as Otornik's knife raised to parry the thrust, Dance swiftly changed the course of his blow and drove straight in!

A feeling of nausea swept over Dance as he felt the keen steel blade bite through flesh and gristle. Otornik screamed and went limp. The knife clattered from his hand and he stumbled to the floor, carrying Dance's knife with him.

Back of him, Dance heard a curse and recognised Worden's voice. He whirled to see Worden, Grindall and the others, standing with their arms in the air, covered by Chuck Osborn's guns.

Dance realized now that Chuck was talking. '. . . and keep 'em high, you scuts out of hell! I'm not taking chances. Keep 'em high, I say! . . . Grindall, open those doors. We're leaving!'

Dance was weary, nearly exhausted. He glanced once at Otornik's silent form, sprawled on the floor, then stepped to Osborn's side.

'You were fast enough for him, Dancer,' Chuck said, his eyes straight ahead.

'I was lucky,' Dance contradicted quietly. 'Did these hombres start something?'

Osborn shook his head. 'I was afeared they might, though, when they saw that Otornik was losing. I've had 'em covered for the past few minutes. Me, I just don't take chances when I'm dealing with snakes . . . You hurt any?'

'My shirt's ripped a mite,' Dance said grimly. 'I've got a scratch on my side, but I don't reckon it amounts to anything. Let's go.'

Grindall had opened the doors. Dance drew on his boots, donned his sombrero, rolled down his sleeves and buckled on his guns and belts. He turned to Worden.

'You hombres can put down your arms now. We're leaving. I'm hoping you'll try to stop us, but I reckon you've got too much sense.'

'You can't pull out too soon to suit me,' Worden snarled.

'I gathered that was your feeling when you arranged this fight,' Dance pointed out. 'I told you before it started it was your fight, all arranged in your mind. Now I'm sure of it.'

'I didn't arrange this fight,' Worden said sullenly, but his eyes didn't meet Dance's. 'You mixed with Otornik and you come out lucky—'

'Luckier than you figured I'd be,' Dance said stern-voiced. 'Don't lie to me, Worden. I

81

know your breed. I haven't got proof of a thing against you right now, but I know I'll get proof—as sure as hell. Just remember, it's still your fight. At the first false move you make, I'll get you. Savvy?'

Worden had no reply for that. Dance and Osborn backed out of the Red Phoenix, their guns in their holsters now, their eyes alert for the first hostile sign, but there was none forthcoming. For the time being, the Red Phoenix occupants were too astounded at the defeat of Otornik to show any immediate belligerency.

Dance and the deputy reached the sidewalk with nothing more being said. Osborn gave vent to a long sigh of relief. 'Thank Gawd, that's over. You had me worried, Dancer. But you come through in elegant style. That's the end of Blade Otornik. Looks like there's a new "best knife in the Southwest" or whatever fool thing it was Otornik called himself.'

Dance shook his head. 'Lord, I was lucky, Chuck. I don't want to be the best knife in the Southwest, or any place else. I don't like knives. It's not my way. It doesn't seem right, somehow. I felt pretty sick when I—well, there at the last.'

'I get you,' Osborn nodded soberly.

Dance formed a tired smile. 'I tell you, we'll go down to your office and tell Sam about it. I'll have him look at this scratch on my ribs. Then we'd better go get that bourbon we started after. I need a drink and I reckon you can stand one.'

'Shucks, my headache is a heap better since I've seen you fight.' And Osborn almost grinned. 'But I can sure use some bourbon, Dancer.'

CHAPTER EIGHT

Two days passed with no incident deserving of mention taking place. Carabina seemed to have quieted down considerably, for which Sheriff Sam Purdy was duly thankful. At the same time, this fact puzzled him. It wasn't natural.

He was standing in the bar at the Cowman's Rest Hotel, having his mid-morning drink with the Dancer. Aside from the two, Jeff Reed, the combination bartender and hotel clerk, was the only man present.

Purdy was gravely shaking his head. 'I don't like it, Jim,' he stated gravely. 'Things is running too smooth.'

' "In time of peace," ' Dancer quoted, ' "prepare for war." '

'That's the idea exactly,' Purdy nodded; 'but I don't know in what direction to prepare. The Red Phoenix has been plumb peaceful since you downed Otornik—by the way, how is that scratch he gave you?'

The Dancer smiled, 'Healing nicely. It didn't amount to anything in the first place, as you know. It doesn't even feel sore, now.'

'You're lucky it wasn't worse. Anyway, you done a good job getting rid of that knife man. News travels around and what you done has had a good effect on the town. Fights and robberies aren't so plentiful as they were. I could almost believe, if I didn't know 'em, that the Grindall and Worden crowd had decided to reform—'

'Not that pair.' Dance shook his head.

'I reckon you're right and we needn't be disappointed if they don't start attending prayer meeting. At the same time, I can't understand why things are so quiet.'

'Perhaps the fact that I'm in Carabina has given Worden and Grindall something to think about,' Dance said quietly.

'You after them two?' Purdy asked.

The Dancer shrugged his lean shoulders. 'I can't say yet, Sam.' He changed the subject. 'Let's have a cigar.'

Jeff Reed rose from the far end of the bar where he had been reading a month-old Kansas City newspaper, and placed an opened box of cigars on the bar. The Dancer and Purdy selected their smokes and lighted up. Reed placed the price of the smokes in his till, then returned to his newspaper.

Purdy puffed furiously for a few moments. His voice, when he finally spoke, came through a cloud of cigar smoke. 'Regardless what yore aims are in Carabina,' he said, 'I'm admittin' frank that I don't know what way to turn next. I can handle open warfare, when it comes, but when the enemy refuses to make any sort of move, I'm blocked complete.'

'Maybe the enemy is licked,' Dance suggested.

Purdy snorted sceptically. 'Yes, and mebbe roast beef comes from hawgs—only it don't . . . Nope, I've been through these peaceful spells before, and they always mean trouble, eventual. Now, if I only knew what Grindall and Worden intended to do next, I could lay plans to stop 'em, but the trouble is, I don't know, and I haven't any way to find out. I'll just have to wait until hell breaks loose again, and then do my level best to rope and hawgtie it.'

'Why don't you,' Dance proposed quietly, 'appoint me a deputy in this county, Sam?'

For a moment the sheriff just stared, then a look of incredulous joy brightened his eyes. 'Jim! Do you mean that? You can't!'

'But I do. Nothing else.' Dance nodded. 'No, believe me, I'm serious. I'm not joshing you. You swear me in as a special deputy and give me a free rein. I won't intrude on Chuck Osborn's authority, of course. All I'd ask of either of you would be cooperation. But it would give me a certain prestige, authority, standing in Carabina.'

'By Hannah! I'll do it,' the sheriff exclaimed. He chuckled. 'I'll appoint you under-sheriff, dam'd if I won't. With you to back me up, we'll make this old town stand around and take notice.'

'We'll do our damndest.' Dance nodded.

Suddenly the sheriff's face dropped. 'But, shucks, Jim, I still don't see just what you'd get out of it.'

The Dancer explained, 'Sam, you want to abolish certain conditions in Carabina. When I've had time to investigate a mite, I may find other conditions here, conditions unknown to you, that *I* want abolished. You've more or less got to take my word for this, as I'm not yet ready to go into details, but you can trust me when I say that I'm on the trail of something big, and that we'll both be working on the side of law and order.'

'Hell, you don't have to explain nothin' to me, Jim . . . C'mon, we'll head down to my office and I'll swear you in, before you have time to change your mind.'

'I'm ready.' Dance smiled at the sheriff's eager manner.

They said *'adiós'* to Jeff Reed and made their way out of the Cowman's Rest bar.

A few minutes later, they were entering the sheriff's office. Deputy Osborn was seated in the shade, at the side wall of the building, but he rose with alacrity when the sheriff called to him to follow them.

In the office, Purdy announced, 'Chuck, luck is breaking our way. Jim has asked to be sworn in as a special deputy.'

Osborn groaned. 'Oh, fiddlesticks! That makes my headache worse'n ever. I should have had my tea, long ago, so as to survive the shock. Now I know there'll be more trouble. Just when my nerves was commencin' to get settled down peaceful too.'

The Dancer smiled. 'Sheriff, I'd sort of like to have Chuck work with me, if possible. Maybe we can drink some tea together.'

Osborn brightened. 'That's a good idea. Misery loves company.'

'I'll do this,' Sam Purdy stated. 'I'll swear in Jim as a special deputy, with power to act as under-sheriff in my absence. Chuck, you'll take orders from Jim, if necessary.'

'No good,' Dance protested promptly. 'How about me taking orders from Chuck? I don't aim to cut in on any man's authority.'

'Aw, you go to hell,' Chuck observed genially. 'I'll be plumb glad to take yore orders, Jim. That means you'll have to do the thinking, which same I admit, frank, will be a big relief. Thinking always was bad for muh nerves, which are more or less shaky and in a delicate condition. I wouldn't be surprised any day now, if I went into a decline and had a nervous breakdown. Just lately I've noticed that every drink I take goes to my stomach. I ain't a well man, a-tall, so, Jim, you'd better

87

shoulder the authority.'

Finally the matter was settled to everyone's satisfaction. The sheriff swore in Dance as under-sheriff and special deputy, with full power to act in his—the sheriff's—absence. After a few minutes' rummaging in his desk, Purdy located a badge of office which he pinned on Dance's vest.

When this business was completed, Osborn walked gravely to one side of the room where a Winchester rifle was suspended on pegs driven into the wall. He took down the rifle, squinted along the sights, then gave a long sigh of satisfaction.

The sheriff's brows knitted. 'What's the idea, Chuck?'

'I'm getting ready to go down to the Red Phoenix and let daylight through Grindall's thick skull,' Chuck stated in dismal accents. 'The only way I know to clean a locality of skunks is with a rifle and no mercy. All's I'm waitin' on, now, is Jim's orders to commence.'

The Dancer smiled. 'Better replace the gun, Chuck. We're not yet ready to start.'

'Oh, shucks,' Chuck growled, 'now that you got a badge you're just like all law officers after all. You sort of remind me of Sam, the way you postpone important matters.'

Disappointedly, the deputy replaced the rifle.

Purdy chuckled. 'Must be nearly time for your tea, ain't it, Chuck?'

'I've give up drinkin' tea,' Osborn mournfully shook his head. 'Tea is too strong for my stomach. I've been thinking of switching to buttermilk, like Tracy Chapman drinks—'

'Like Chapman drinks when he can get it,' Purdy growled. 'The mealy-mouthed coyote. Not that there's anything against his drinkin' buttermilk—I like it myself—but you'd think this was a country of dairy farms around here, 'stead of a stock-raisin' community. Two or three times now, I've seen him get plumb peeved 'cause the restaurants and bars don't stock buttermilk reg'lar.'

'Buttermilk? Chapman?' Dance said thoughtfully. 'That gives me an idea.'

'What sort of an idea?' Purdy asked.

'Some ten or fifteen years back,' Dance explained. 'I remember a man named Chapman being traced and caught through his liking for buttermilk.'

'Where was this?' Purdy queried.

'Eastern Texas—Beaumont was the town where they caught him.'

'What had he done?' Chuck wanted to know.

'As I remember it,' Dance said slowly, 'he was quite a notorious forger.'

Purdy asked, 'Do you figure we're both talking about the same Chapman?'

Dance shrugged his lean shoulders. 'I couldn't say. I was pretty much of a slicker, those days. I just happened to remember reading in the papers about the case. I don't even recollect the fellow's first name. It might have been Tracy. I do remember it was Chapman, though, and that he was sentenced to prison.'

'Maybe that explains something,' the sheriff said gravely; 'something I was never quite sure on before.'

'In what way?'

'When Tracy Chapman first came to Carabina,' Purdy responded, 'he let on to be an Easterner, out here for his health. He was pretty pasty-looking, and didn't appear particularly healthy. His complexion always did look like prison pallor to me, though I never mentioned my ideas to anyone.'

Dance nodded and said thoughtfully, 'Hutch Worden served a prison sentence. He and Chapman are friendly. Perhaps they met in prison. Did they appear to know each other when Chapman first came to Carabina?'

Purdy shook his head. 'Nope, Chapman came here and told folks he was looking for peace and quiet. Then, sort of gradual, he drifted in with Worden and Grindall. He spends quite a bit of time at Grindall's Bow-Knot Ranch and claims to be resting up. What do you think of the situation, Jim?'

Dance shrugged his shoulders again. 'Off-hand, I don't like to say. I don't like it, of course, but I won't make any statements until my ideas commence dovetailing better than they do right now.'

'Want I should take Chapman up on suspicion, Jim?' Osborn said sourly, trying to keep the eagerness out of his voice.

'Suspicion of what, Chuck?' Dance asked.

'That is up to you. Remember, you were to do the thinking.'

The Dancer smiled, shook his head. 'We'll let things drift along as they are at present, Chuck. Chapman is the least of our troubles . . . Say, do you feel like taking a ride?'

'Sure. Where to?'

Dance said, 'We might take a trip out to the Bow-Knot.'

'I'm ready any time you say.'

Purdy put in, 'What do you want to go to the Bow-Knot for, Jim?' The sheriff looked curiously at his new deputy.

'I'd sort of like to give a look-see around.'

'Just packed full of information, ain't you?' Purdy said ironically.

'Yeah,' Dance smiled, 'but not passing any out.' Then, noticing the look of disappointment on Purdy's face, Dance went on, 'Sam, I told you when I asked to be sworn in as a deputy, that you'd have to trust me to do things my own way. At times, I may do things a bit high-handed, without taking time to explain things to you. When I act, I'm right likely to move first and explain later—mebbe. I'm taking the course that seems best to me, and if I come out on the winning end, you'll share in a victory that's a heap more important than just taming the rougher element in Carabina—'

'Say, Jim,' Purdy interrupted, 'you don't have to make any excuses to me. I've said before and I'll say again that I trust you from hell to breakfast. I was just curious, that's all.'

Dance nodded, smiling, 'I hope it won't be much longer before your curiosity is satisfied.'

Osborn said impatiently, 'C'mon, Jim let's get started.'

'Can you stir up a horse for me?' Dance asked Osborn. 'How about the livery down the street? Are there any good ponies there, or are they all crowbaits?'

'The Blue Star Livery is all right,' the sheriff cut in, 'but I've got a better idea. I've got an extra hawss boardin' there. Bought him off'n a broke cowpuncher who came here a coupla months back. I didn't have any use for another horse, but he looked right good to me, and I couldn't resist him. Little black gelding. There's rig, bridle and spurs at the livery, too. That horse is just gettin' fat from no exercise. I'd be plumb appreciative if you'd take him.'

'Thanks, Sam. That's mighty decent of you.'

'You'll be doing me a favor if you work him a mite. No thanks necessary. Take him and welcome.'

'I'll be glad to borrow your horse, Sam.'

Dance and Osborn left the sheriff's office

and walked along the street, until they had reached the post office which was located in a small frame building.

'I want to stop in here a minute,' Dance said. 'I'll be right out.'

Osborn waited in front of the post office, while Dance disappeared inside. In a minute or so he emerged, a frown on his face.

Osborn said, 'What's wrong? Didn't she write to you?'

Dance forced a faint smile. 'I wasn't looking for a letter from a girl, Chuck. I was hoping for news, though.'

'And it didn't come, eh?'

Again, Dance shook his head. 'In one way, I hardly expected it to come. On the other hand, it might have.'

'Does that affect *us* in any way—or just you?'

'It means that we get that horse of Sam's and ride to the Bow-Knot,' Dance evaded.

'And if you had received a letter, we wouldn't have gone to the Bow-Knot, eh?'

'I didn't say that. Either way,' Dance said cryptically, 'we'd have made that ride. Is your horse at the livery stable, too?'

Osborn nodded his head, thinking hard over Dance's words. 'I don't know what you're expecting to find at the Bow-Knot,' he said at last, 'but I'm hopin' for action.'

*　　　*　　　*

It was about two-thirty in the afternoon when Dance and Osborn sighted the Bow-Knot Ranch buildings. They had taken time to eat dinner in Carabina, before leaving. Then, the sheriff's horse at the livery stable had been inclined to buck when Dance settled into the saddle. The gentling down of the spirited animal had required a little more time, but once the two men were on their way to the Bow-Knot, Dance was forced to agree that Purdy hadn't exaggerated in his praise of the little black gelding. As Dance said, 'He's all horse, Chuck, and looks like he'd be a staying fool when it comes to endurance and speed. I reckon I'll have to try and buy him from Sam.'

The Bow-Knot was situated on the side of a gently sloping rise of land, and consisted of ranch-house, cook shanty, mess-house, windmill, corrals, barns, stables and so on. It looked like a prosperous outfit. The buildings were in a good state of repair and had recently received a fresh coat of whitewash.

Now and then, as Dance and Osborn drew nearer, they saw small bunches of Hereford cows, branded with the Bow-Knot design.

'How many cows does Grindall run?' Dance asked.

Osborn reined his pony slightly nearer Dance's mount, then replied, 'Are you referring to his own critters, or other folks'?'

'Tosses a wide loop, does he?'

'I wish I could prove it,' Chuck growled. 'A lot of us suspect him of rustling, but nobody has ever been able to catch him at it. He sold a large number of cows right after his wife died, and has never bought any new herds that I know of, so he can't have many cows left on his range. At that, Grindall makes a right nice shipment from time to time. He always seems to have plenty of money.'

'Maybe his money comes from the Red Phoenix.'

'I ain't convinced all of it does,' Osborn said doggedly. 'Of course, he makes good profits out of that honkeytonk, but—'

'Maybe,' Dance cut in, 'he has other ways of making money.'

'Meaning just what?'

Dance laughed softly. 'That's something we'll have to discover, Chuck.'

Osborn nodded gloomily. The two men rode on in silence, their horses kicking up small clouds of dust along the trail which was bordering on either side with grazing lands, now and then dotted with clumps of sage, cacti or mesquite.

When the two deputies rode into the yard, there wasn't a soul to be seen. A few horses, in the saddlers' corral, provided the only movement about the place.

'This is damn' funny,' Osborn said suspiciously. He raised his voice, 'Hey, Bow-Knot! Where's everybody? You got company-y-y!'

But there came no voice in reply. An unusual silence hung about the place. Dance and Osborn dismounted and started toward the bunk-house.

'We'll look into this,' Dance stated, puzzled. 'It seems like the cook would be around, some place anyway.'

'Mebbe they've all been overtook by the black plague and died sudden.' Osborn was almost smiling when he spoke the words. 'Wouldn't that be grand news?'

The bunk-house door stood open and proved on inspection to be empty. There weren't even any blankets in the double tier of bunks along one wall.

'Cripes!' Osborn said. 'There ain't even a saddle around. This ain't right. Something's happened. It looks like everybody had packed up and lit out right sudden.'

The Dancer was walking idly about the bunk-house. 'What's this?' he said suddenly, picking a sheet of paper, covered with writing, from a table under one of the bunk-house windows. He glanced quickly at the writing, then smiled.

'Here,' Dance said, holding out the sheet of paper, 'this explains everything—nearly. The crew has resigned and lit a shuck away from here.'

'T'hell you say.' Chuck looked startled.

'I'm telling you.'

'But why should Grindall's crew resign—in a body?'

'If you'll read this note, left by Grindall's foreman, maybe you'll understand.' He handed the sheet of paper to Chuck.

Chuck read:

Dear Nick: We have all decided to high-tail it down to Mexico. The Dancer being in Carabina don't look so good to us. Buck knew of him down in Texas, and Buck says he's a heller on wheels when he starts shaking lead out of his guns. It looks like the finish of your game, if he is after you and Hutch. Anyway, we ain't going to stay and run chances on catching a long term in the pen. I would ride in and tell you this, but you are due out here today anyhow, so it won't make no difference. We took our wages due out of the money which you left with me to get that fencing. I know you won't like it when I tell you that, because we took two months' wages in advance, but we figure you owe us that much. Don't set nobody trailing us, because if we get caught, we will tell the Dancer what we know. If that happens it will be your finish. Yr. obedient servant,

ED. MALLARE,
Ex-foreman,
Bow-Knot Ranch.

Osborn looked up from the paper. 'Well,' he

exploded, 'I'll be damned!'

Dance smiled. 'Your obedient servant. Isn't that funny?'

Osborn nodded. 'It won't be funny to Grindall. The yellow skunks, Jim, you've plumb scared 'em off. What a rep you must have back in Texas!'

'Do you happen to know,' Dance said, 'who this Buck is who claims to know me?'

'Sure. Buck Fenell. He was one of the Bow-Knot punchers.'

Dance's brow furrowed in thought. 'Buck Fenell,' he repeated slowly. Suddenly his face cleared. 'Sure enough. Buck Fenell. I remember him now. He was a would-be-hellraiser down around San'tone a few years back. I took him in one time when I was a Ranger. He had an idea he was tough, but there was more blow and brag to the man than nerve.'

'Well, he sure learned his lesson. Buck certainly made it plain to his pards, and impressed it on 'em, that you wa'n't to be monkeyed with. They've all cleared out to avoid the storm they reckon is on the way.'

'And robbed their boss into the bargain. Two months' wages in advance. Nice loyal crowd. There's nothing wrong with that Mallare's nerve, anyway—only he hasn't the right kind of nerve.'

'I always did suspect him of being a thief. Now I'm plumb shore of it . . . Well, what do we do next? Get on the trail of these skunks and learn what they know about Worden and Grindall?'

Dance shook his head. 'I don't reckon. They've got a long start. They'll be in Mexico before we could catch up. There'd be too much red tape to untangle before you could arrest 'em down there.'

'And besides,' Osborn put in, 'you wouldn't know what to arrest 'em for, would you?'

Dance didn't reply to that question.

'Chuck,' he said, a moment later, 'you stay outside and keep an eye open for anybody coming. I'm going to snoop around these buildings a trifle and see can I pick up any sort of sign.'

'What kind of sign?'

'I'm not yet sure. I'll keep this note. We'll deliver it to Grindall at the Red Phoenix, unless we meet him on the trail, on our return to town. The note says he was due out here, today.'

'Go to it. I'll watch. If I see anybody coming this way, I'll whistle.'

Dance nodded and left the bunk-house. He headed first for the ranch-house, and, finding the door unlocked, he stepped inside to the kitchen. From the kitchen he went through every room in the house. All of them were empty, except for furniture, and with one exception showed no traces of recent occupancy. This particular room he judged to have been Polly Loomis', when she lived at the Bow-Knot.

From the house, Dance went to the other buildings on the property, and entered each building. He found no more than he had in the ranch-house proper.

Finally he emerged into the open air again, a look of disappointment on his face.

'Didn't find what you were looking for, eh?' Osborn commented. He had mounted his pony and sat in the saddle, keeping a keen eye on the trail from Carabina.

Dance shook his head. 'Not a-tall.'

'What were you lookin' for?'

Dance didn't appear to hear the question. He asked, 'Does Grindall own any other buildings that you know of, Chuck?'

'The Red Phoenix—with Worden.'

'I don't mean that.'

Osborn shook his head, then, 'Well, there's some line camps scattered around the Bow-Knot holdin's.'

'H'mm . . . Well, maybe we'll investigate those camps, one of these days. I reckon we'd better slope back to town now.'

'Dang it all,' Osborn said mournfully, 'I was hoping we might have a little ruckus here— just to sort of calm my nerves. Dang you, Jim! I shore wish yore reputation hadn't traveled so fast.'

'So do I,' Dance said seriously. 'I'd have liked to have had a talk with Buck Fenell and see just what he knew about Grindall and Worden. Well, we'd better ride.'

Osborn handed the reins of Dance's horse over to him. Dance climbed into the saddle, wheeled his mount and the two riders loped out of the deserted ranch yard.

CHAPTER NINE

The Dancer caught sight of Sheriff Purdy as he and Chuck rode into Carabina. 'Hiyuh, Sam!' Dance called.

Purdy glanced around, saw Osborn and Dance reining their ponies toward the sidewalk. He came up to them, walking fast.

'Where you been, what you been doing, what do you know?' the sheriff asked all in a single breath, as the ponies came to a stop.

'We ain't done nothin', or found nothin',' Chuck growled before Dance could reply. 'This country has gone plumb haywire as regards excitement—or the lack of it.'

Dance said quietly, 'Well, we made the ride to the Bow-Knot. There wasn't anybody there. I went all through the buildings, but couldn't find a thing.'

'Nobody there—' the sheriff commenced, then paused and said abruptly, 'Do you mean, Jim, you searched the premises without a search warrant?'

'Nothing else,' Dance smiled.

'Good Lord, man! If Grindall learns this, he'll have the county authorities down on us—'

'Don't forget, Sam, I warned you when you made me a deputy, that I'd do things my own way. If I've overstepped your authority a bit, I'll resign this badge at once—'

'Forget it,' Purdy shook his head. 'It's all right, Jim. You keep that badge and act as you see fit. The surprise of going through a place without a search warrant sort of swept me off'n my feet for a moment.'

'Anyway,' Dance said, 'you've nothing to worry about. Grindall won't make trouble—if he does, just remember that I can handle him. I've got a higher authority than this deputy badge and if necessary I'll make use of it, if I have to. Only, for the time being, I'd rather Worden and Grindall didn't know what brought me here.'

'Sure. Do as you think best, Jim. I'm glad to have you backing me up. The news has got around that I've added you to my side, and it has had a good effect already . . . By the way, what did you expect to find at the Bow-Knot?'

'You haven't shown any curiosity yet,' Dance evaded the sheriff's question with a smile, 'regarding the resignation of Grindall's crew.'

'Great Scott! Has the crew quit the Bow-Knot? You mentioned nobody was there, but I thought you meant—'

'This will explain.' Dance took from his pocket the note written by Grindall's ex-foreman. 'We thought maybe we'd meet Grindall riding to the Bow-Knot, on our return here, but I guess he hasn't started yet.'

Purdy accepted the note, read it. In a few minutes he returned the paper to Dance, saying with a frown, 'Do you think this was left for Grindall?'

'Certain of it,' Dance nodded. 'Who else would it be meant for?'

'I was thinkin',' Purdy said slowly, 'that it might be a bluff of some sort.'

'Why a bluff?'

Purdy shook his head. 'I just don't know. It's beyond me. What you aimin' to do with this note?'

'Hand it to Grindall,' Dance smiled. 'When I see how he accepts the news I'll know whether it's a bluff or not.'

'Well, all I got to say,' Purdy chuckled, 'is that you got your enemies buffaloed, if they'll clear out like it says on the note. What do you know about this Buck Fenell?'

Dance told him, adding, 'Fenell's word must carry a heap of weight with his pards. Either that, or they've got guilty consciences.'

'That's something that's understood by everybody that knows that crew,' Chuck Osborn growled. 'That Ed Mallare—Grindall's foreman—was a mean-looking hombre, and I never did trust him any. If he's gone for good,

103

I'm damn' glad of it.'

Dance turned back to the sheriff, 'Where you heading, Sam?'

'No place in particular. Just strolling around.'

'Looking for trouble?'

'Looking for trouble to stop, if possible.'

'What's up?'

'Nothing in particular.'

'You got something on your mind, Sam Purdy.'

'Well, yes, I have,' Purdy admitted with a sigh. 'Dick Loomis is in town—you know—Polly's brother. He's sort of hot-headed and I don't want the boy to get hurt.'

'Explain yourself.'

Purdy explained, 'Well, it's been sort of rumored around that Dick is out to get Grindall. You see, the news finally percolated out to the Rafter-N, where Dick's been working, of what happened at the Red Phoenix, the other night—you know, when you helped Polly out of that scrape and shot Taggert—'

'I know when you mean. Go ahead.'

'Well,' Purdy resumed 'to make a long story short, Dick hit the ceiling, when he heard about it—or so a couple of his friends told me. He quit his job and come to town. I understand he swears Grindall has either got to give him and Polly shares in the Bow-Knot, on legal paper, or Polly will get the ranch all to herself.'

'Meaning?'

'Meaning,' Purdy said uneasily, 'that young Dick is willin' to stand trial for killing Grindall. If Grindall dies, the Bow-Knot automatically goes to Dick and Polly. Grindall deserves shooting, no doubt of that, but on the other hand, Dick might—'

'If you ask me,' Chuck cut in, 'I think a jury would free Dick and vote him a medal.'

' 'T'aint like you, Chuck,' Purdy observed, 'to speculate so optimistic-like. Personally, I think Dick would swing. Grindall's friends would see that honest men weren't on the jury. The boy would be tried by a bunch of men who would have their minds made up before the case opened. Don't forget, Worden still swings a lot of influence in this country. If Dick was to kill Grindall, it would be called murder, shore as hell!'

'Not if it was a fair fight, Sam,' Dance contradicted. 'From what I've heard of Dick he's not the boy to shoot Grindall in the back.'

'It's the only way Dick could get Grindall,' Purdy said gloomily. 'He wouldn't have a dog's chance against Grindall's guns. Grindall is too fast, too experienced, for Dick. Grindall knows that and has nothing to fear. Dick knows it too, but his hot temper is likely to run away with his judgment. In consequence, Dick is li'ble to meet up with an early grave.'

'Has Dick told you he aims to kill Grindall?'

Dance asked.

Purdy shook his head. 'No, he ain't—but I've never heard he wouldn't try, neither. Me, I'm plumb worried. I couldn't bear to look Polly in the eye, if I ever allowed that young 'un to be hurt.'

It was growing dark now. Lights were springing into being along the thoroughfare. The sun had long since dropped behind the distant peaks of the Fuente Range.

Abruptly, Osborn announced, 'I'm hungry. Who's for chow?'

'I'll eat later,' Purdy said. 'You two run along.'

'I've got to give this note to Grindall first,' Dance smiled, 'and see how he takes this news that his crew has pulled out and left him flat.'

Dance and Osborn reined their ponies back to the center of the roadway and in a few minutes had dismounted at the livery stable where they left the horses to be taken care of.

From the livery they proceeded to the Red Phoenix, which was already agleam with lights, though it was too early for much business.

Nick Grindall was just descending the steps from his place, and had headed for the hitchrack, when he glanced around and saw Dance and Osborn approaching. A black scowl contorted his face, then he continued on toward his saddled horse.

By this time, Dance and Osborn had drawn abreast of the Red Phoenix.

106

Dance said, 'Heading for the Bow-Knot, Grindall?'

Grindall whirled around, then stepped back to the sidewalk. Dance saw, now, that Grindall had been drinking. The man's face was flushed, his eyes red-rimmed.

'What in hell is it to you?' Grindall growled.

'Figured I might save you a trip, in case you aimed to see your foreman.'

'Yeah? How you figuring you got a right to interest yourself in my business?'

The Dancer laughed softly. 'Grindall, you try and work out a way to keep me from getting interested in your business.'

Grindall sobered. He looked suspiciously at Dance, then, 'What in hell you driving at, Dance?'

For reply, Dance extracted from his pocket the note of resignation, and passed it to Grindall. Again a suspicious look crossed the man's face. He glanced sharply at Osborn, then back to the Dancer.

'Oh, shucks, Grindall,' Chuck said wearily, 'read what that note says. We're not your kind—the kind that pulls a gun on a man when he's occupied with his business letters. Read the note, then do your thinkin' and actin.'

Grindall moved across the sidewalk where he could stand in the light from one of the Red Phoenix windows, and unfolded the note. Suddenly, as he read, a curse broke from his lips. He crumpled the note in his hand, then unfolded it and read its contents a second time.

Abruptly, he turned and came striding back to face Dance.

'Where'd you get this note?' Grindall demanded.

'From the table in your bunk-house,' Dance replied easily.

'Did you read it?'

Dance smiled. 'I reckon I did.'

'Snappy as hell, ain't you?' Grindall sneered.

'I have to be, sometimes—especially as my name is mentioned on that paper.'

'That crew is a bunch of cowardly rats, Dancer,' Grindall toned down his manner. 'Just because you had something on one of my men, is no sign you got anything on me. I don't know what Ed Mallare is referrin' to when he writes that he'll tell you what he knows about me—'

'No?' Dance smiled sceptically. 'What you getting so nervous about, Grindall? You seem to be a mite bothered.'

'We-ell,' Grindall said uncertainly, 'I—I thought he meant that—well, that is, you see—I—I—' Beads of perspiration commenced to form on the man's forehead.

'You needn't bother to explain, Grindall,' Dance smiled. 'I don't claim to have anything on you—yet. I brought in that note just to save you a trip. If your conscience is clear, so is

108

mine.'

'Oh, yes, uh-huh. Well, thanks—' Grindall paused, growing angry as a new thought penetrated his mind. 'Just what was you doing out to the Bow-Knot, anyway?' he demanded, his face clouding darkly.

'Just looking around,' Dance said airily. 'Chuck and I were riding past, and we just thought we'd drop in casual-like.'

'Casual-like, eh?' Grindall snapped. 'It don't go down, Dance. You had a purpose in stopping at the Bow-Knot.'

'Oh, hell,' in tired accents from Osborn, 'we might as well tell him, Jim. You see, Nick, we was on the hunt for a bunch of prime Circle-Bar steers that have disappeared—'

'Well, don't look for 'em on my place,' Grindall rasped, though he seemed suddenly relieved.

'We sort of look every place,' Osborn drawled.

Grindall swore under his breath, turned to Dance. 'I know, I know,' he said hotly. 'Some of the stock men around here think I don't get all my cattle honest, but I do. Dancer, you been hired to look for stock by the Circle-Bar?'

'I didn't say so,' Dance said quietly.

'Well, I don't give a damn either way,' Grindall jerked out. 'I ain't got any Circle-Bar steers on my holdings, and you're just wasting time, if you've been suspicioning me. From now on, you keep off'n the Bow-Knot—'

'Me, I don't usually waste much time,' Dance drawled. 'If I ever do start concentratin' on you, Grindall, you'll realize I'm not wasting any time.'

'Keep away from the Bow-Knot,' Grindall repeated angrily.

'And supposing I don't?'

'You're liable to contact a bad case of lead-poisonin', Dancer!'

'That sounds like a threat, Grindall.'

The Dancer's eyes narrowed to thin slits now.

Grindall rasped, 'You can take it exactly as it sounds.'

'Want to start anything now,' Dance challenged quietly.

Grindall paused, temper rising again. He fought to hold himself in check. He was remembering Worden's words regarding the Dancer's prowess with a six-shooter. Grindall didn't quite believe Worden. In his heart he felt quite sure he could beat Dance to the draw. Still Worden had admitted being a bit cautious where facing the Dancer was concerned.

Suddenly, without replying, Grindall wheeled around and started for the interior of the Red Phoenix, to get Worden's advice before proceeding further. He was halfway up the wide steps in front of the building, when Dance spoke again.

'Want to start anything now, Grindall?' Dance repeated softly.

The cool taunting tones in Dance's voice acted like a red rag to a bull on Grindall's already taut nerves. He saw that passers-by had paused to listen. There were men standing on the porch of the Red Phoenix, waiting curiously to see what Grindall would do. Grindall didn't dare lose prestige by backing down now. But still he hesitated, midway to the entrance to the big honkytonk, his face purple with rage.

And then, a third time came the Dancer's goading words, 'Want to try anything now, Grindall?'

Grindall cursed, flung himself in a mad rush down the steps to confront Dance. Two yards away from Dance he came to a halt.

'Not this minute, Dancer,' he snarled, 'but I'll get you when you ain't got Deputy Osborn around to back your play.'

'When?' Dance snapped the one word.

Grindall was shaking with anger. He half choked on his reply. 'Dancer, this town ain't big enough to hold both of us. I'm giving you twenty-four hours to get out. If I see you in Carabina after that, pull your hardware. I'll be after you with guns smokin'! Remember, twenty-four hours is all you've got.'

The Dancer laughed softly. 'Grindall,' he drawled, 'twenty-four hours is a long time to wait. Can't you shorten that limit to minutes?'

111

But Grindall was too full of rage to speak further. He wheeled about and rushed back into the Red Phoenix.

CHAPTER TEN

The Dancer laughed softly, drew a watch from his pocket. 'Just exactly seven-fifteen,' after consulting the instrument. 'Twenty-four hours from now I've got to be on my way.'

'You leavin'?' Osborn looked startled.

'What do you think?' Dance drawled.

'Grindall is lightnin' fast,' Osborn pointed out in sober tones.

'I don't doubt it.'

'He's tricky. He might drygulch you.'

'That's just my hard luck if he does. If I can't keep my eyes open, I'll have no one to blame but myself.'

'You'll have to keep your eyes open. It won't be a fair, face-to-face fight. He'll hide around the corner of a building. You won't have a dog's chance, if he can work things his way.'

The Dancer laughed. 'I've never yet been run out of any town,' he drawled, 'and I'm not intending to allow a skunk like Grindall to inaugurate any such custom. I'll be staying.'

'Hell, I knew you would, Jim.'

'I'll be here long after Grindall has left,' Dance said quietly, 'so we won't worry now

112

about anything that may happen twenty-four hours from now . . . Let's go eat. My stomach is commencing to wonder if my throat has been cut.'

Chuck Osborn suggested the dining-room at the Cowman's Rest Hotel, as being the 'best place to get a bite.'

The two men started along the sidewalk, both a trifle quiet, both thinking of the recent encounter with Nick Grindall and of the results that the next meeting might bring forth.

They were passing a small 'dobe building when two figures emerged from the shadows. One of the figures spoke, 'Señor Dance.'

Dance and Osborn halted. The young Mexican who had shadowed Dobe Liston the morning Dance left on the freight for Carabina, emerged from the gloom, followed by his partner.

'*Coma'sta*, Pascual,' Dance greeted, shaking hands 'and Juan, too. Glad to see you.' He introduced the two to Osborn, then asked, 'When did you get in?'

'We come here not so long ago. The conductor of the freight that carried you and Liston, allowed us to ride in his caboose—'

'Liston never got here.'

'But, *señor*,' Pascual insisted, 'with my own eyes I saw him climb to the box car at the same time you left. I tried to stop him, but my pig of a gunhand failed to hold my weapon of the best steadiness and I missed my shot.'

113

'I didn't,' Dance said soberly. 'I shot it out with him, on the way here, the next day.' He explained briefly what had happened, to the accompaniment of many exclamations in Spanish from the two Mexicans.

'Then,' Juan said downheartedly, 'there was no need of our coming. We had hoped to be of assistance. We should have stayed at home with Mateo and eaten his woman's *tortillas*.'

'I'm glad you're here,' Dance said warmly. 'There will be work for you, I think.'

'At once?' Pascual asked hopefully.

'At once,' Dance nodded. 'Go to a place called the Red Phoenix. Ask for the Señor Nick Grindall. Tell him, on the way from Chihuahua, you encountered one Buck Fenell, who told you Grindall required *vaqueros* to work the cows.' Dance had Osborn add a short description of Fenell.

'*Si*, Señor Dance.'

'I'm not sure that Grindall will hire you, but if he does, keep your eyes and ears open.'

'*Si*, Señor Dance.'

'If he doesn't hire you, come to me again, when no one is near. You have money to live?'

'Enough, Señor Dance.'

'*Adiós*,' Dance said briefly and turned away.

'*Vaya con Dios*,' the Mexicans replied in unison, and melted into the darkness, between buildings.

* * *

114

It was drawing near the close of the meal hour, when Dance and Osborn entered the dining-room in the Cowman's Rest Hotel. The Mexican waiter who was employed there was just removing dishes from several of the tables. Only one table was occupied, and Dance noticed that the occupants were Polly Loomis and a young fellow who looked so much like the girl that he was instantly recognizable as her brother Dick.

Polly saw Dance and Chuck enter the dining-room and waved for them to join them. Osborn, of course, was already acquainted with the boy.

'We're just starting to eat,' Polly laughed. 'We might as well make it a party . . . Dick,' to her brother as Dance drew near, 'this is Jim Dance.' Then to Dance, 'I've been telling Dick about you.'

Dick Loomis rose and gripped Dance's hand. 'I'm mighty glad to know you, Jim Dance,' he said sincerely. 'I sort of reckon I'm in your debt a heap. Polly has told me what you did for her and—'

'Shuks,' Dance smiled, 'forget it, boy. I just happened to be there when affairs started coming to a boil and—'

'I'm forgetting nothing,' Dick said soberly. 'I'm going to do some squaring up with Nick Grindall myself.'

The Dancer and Osborn sat down and

115

ordered supper from the Mexican waiter. Polly tried to make the conversation light and cheery during the meal, and Osborn and Dance did their part to help out, but young Dick Loomis ate in moody silence.

While Dance talked he was scrutinising Dick closely. Dance recognised Dick's type— young, high-strung, impulsive and quick-tempered. Dick had doffed working togs for sober black, white collar, shirt and tie, though once, when his coat fell open, Dance noticed a gun-belt about the boy's middle. His hair was blond, though a trifle darker than Polly's. He had retained his cowboy boots and his roll-brim sombrero of gray hung on a hook on the nearby wall.

They were nearly through the meal when Polly said to Dance, 'Dick was feeling rather foolish when he first arrived in Carabina, today.'

The Dancer smiled. 'How come?'

'I'm still feeling thataway,' Dick said moodily, 'if you want to call it foolish. I don't agree that it is foolish. What I'm getting at, I feel that Grindall requires killing. I figure I'm the hombre to do it.'

The Dancer shook his head. 'It seems to me, Dick, there should be other ways of getting your rights.' He spoke calmly. 'Killing is bad business, boy, and should be avoided when possible. A man's death isn't a nice thing to have on your conscience.'

116

'I'll get him in fair fight,' Dick persisted, his smouldering eyes burning into Dance's.

'It still isn't a nice thing to have on your mind,' Dance said soberly, 'whether it's a fair fight or not; sometimes these things are forced on a man and he kills in self-defense, but it doesn't make him feel any easier in his thoughts. Whether you killed Grindall in a fair fight or not, it would still be killing—'

'That's exactly what I've been telling Dick,' Polly broke in. 'Why not take the matter up with a good lawyer—'

'No lawyer can square what happened at the Red Phoenix the other night,' Dick said hotly. 'When I think of Grindall proposing marriage to Polly, well, it makes my blood boil—'

'Oh, Dick,' Polly's voice was almost a wail, 'please forget that. It doesn't matter one way or the other, now. I don't blame you for wanting what is ours in the Bow-Knot property, but Grindall's proposal is something we should laugh at. As to the Bow-Knot problem, I doubt whether a court case would give us what is rightfully ours. At the same time, you might try seeing a lawyer if it would ease your mind, Dick.'

The boy didn't reply at once. He realized the good common sense of Polly's advice, but, youngster-like refused to concede anything to a sister. 'That's what I planned to do at first,' he finally admitted reluctantly, 'but after thinking things over I can't see the sense of

117

wasting court fees and a lawyer on a skunk like Grindall when a slug of lead will do the business faster and less expensively—'

'Oh, Dick, that sounds foolish,' Polly exclaimed impatiently. 'You should know that as well as I.'

'It's dang good sense,' he retorted hotly. 'There's nothing would give me more pleasure than to rub out that skunk. Polly, have you forgotten how he treated mother?'

The girl's eyes grew moist. She bit her lip. The Dancer saw she was too choked up to speak for a minute, and he took up her argument. 'Polly's right, Dick. That is foolish talk. Killing in a good many cases means a prison sentence at best, or a hanging. You're young. You've got a heap of life ahead of you. You'll realize, some day, that Polly is talking sense—'

'I'll take a prison sentence or a hanging gladly,' young Loomis said hotly, 'for the satisfaction of finishing Grindall. I'll have double satisfaction in the thought that his death would give Polly the Bow-Knot—'

'Oh, Dick,' Polly cried impulsively, 'don't you see I don't want the ranch on such terms? I'd kill Grindall myself, before I'd let you do such a thing. You've spoken of mother. She put a lot of faith in you, Dick. Do you think she'd like to see you in prison? How do you suppose she'd feel, if—'

The girl paused, swallowing hard. Tears

welled into her eyes. There ensued an awkward silence. Chuck Osborn tried to cover the awkwardness of the moment by saying, 'Seems like this is a rather murderous gathering. First, Dick, then Polly, seems to be craving Grindall's blood. Well, I'll tell you folks that neither one of you will get the chance to kill him.'

'What do you mean?' Polly asked.

Dance frantically signalled Osborn not to say anything further, but Chuck failed to see the signal.

'Why it looks,' Chuck explained, 'as though Dance will get first crack at that snake.'

'No!' Polly exclaimed.

'Yes,' from Osborn. 'We met Grindall down the street a few minutes back and he lost his head. He gave Jim twenty-four hours to get out of Carabina, or take the results—'

'I don't reckon it will amount to anything,' Dance said quietly. He explained briefly what had taken place, without going into details, and added, 'Grindall had been drinking more than was good for him and he lost his head. After he's sobered up, he'll change his mind about wanting to gun me out of Carabina.'

'But suppose he doesn't?' Polly looked concerned.

'In that case,' Dance drawled, 'I'll just have to tuck my tail between my legs and run for cover.'

The laugh that followed Dance's words

eased the situation. Even Dick brightened a trifle. Immediately afterward, he sobered again, saying, 'I'm already in your debt, Jim Dance. Maybe I can fix things so Grindall won't have a chance to carry out his twenty-four hour threat.'

'You mean, take up my fight?' Dance asked.

'Exactly.' The young fellow's face was serious.

Dance smiled. 'Hands off, Dick. No cutting in on my game. You've got troubles of your own. Anything I do, now that I'm deputy of Carabina, will be done legally. You keep out of this. Just remember, I'm getting first whack at Grindall.'

Within a few minutes, supper was concluded. The three men matched two-bit pieces to see who'd pay for the meal. Osborn lost. Dick remained behind with Osborn while the Mexican waiter made change. Dance accompanied Polly through the side door leading from the dining-room to the street.

On the sidewalk, Polly asked, 'Jim, will you really have to shoot Grindall?'

'Maybe,' Dance's voice was non-committal. 'Maybe he'll shoot me.'

'Do you think Dick will try to kill him?'

Dance considered the girl's question, then spoke truthfully, 'To be frank, Polly, he might, if we don't keep an eye on him. I know his type. He doesn't stop to reason. Maybe I'll be able to fix things so he won't get a chance to face Grindall. Now, don't you worry any.'

'You mean, by killing Grindall yourself?'

The Dancer didn't answer that. The girl repeated her words. The Dancer's steady gaze met her eyes. She didn't look away. In the half-gloom of the street her eyes were luminous, appealing. The Dancer's voice was a trifle unsteady, as he asked, 'Would it make a great deal of difference if I had to kill him?'

Impulsively, the girl's hand went out to him. 'Not so much difference,' and her words didn't falter, 'as it would make if he killed Dick . . . or you.'

'Why me?'

But this time it was the girl who seemed at a loss for words. They heard Osborn and Dick at the doorway of the hotel. The girl pressed Dance's hand hard, then turned away.

Dance's words just reached her ears, 'Trust me, Polly. I'll do my best to keep Dick out of trouble.'

The girl swung back to face him, her eyes full of mingled worry and gratitude. 'I'm not asking you,' and her words brought a certain thrill to the Dancer's heart, 'to run any risks. I don't want you hurt, either . . . Jim.'

Osborn and Dick came up at that moment.

'Where now?' Dick asked.

'I've got to go feed a hoosegow full of hungry prisoners,' Chuck said, 'and give Sam a chance to get away for his supper. I'm 'way overdue now. I'll see you folks later.'

'I reckon,' Dance smiled, 'this is as good a chance as any for me to get acquainted with Dick. Maybe Dick and I can sort of pal around together, tonight.'

'That sounds,' Polly laughed, 'as though I were to be left out of things. Well, you two can take me to Ma Morley's first, then do what you choose . . . Where are you staying tonight?'

'I've got a room at the hotel,' Dick replied. 'We'll walk with you to your boardinghouse, Polly, then you can go to bed like a good girl.'

'But can I sleep?' she eyed him gravely.

The Dancer caught the import of her words. 'You can sleep,' he told her confidently. 'This isn't Grindall's night to be shot.'

Dick smiled nervously. 'Sure, sis, don't you worry about me. You get your sleep. I promise not to pull a gun tonight—'

'And maybe,' Dance put in, 'we can get a promise for tomorrow, too. Dick isn't nearly so riled now, as he was at first.'

'Aw, shucks,' Dick said rather boyishly, 'I know I was brewing a heap of war when I rode into Carabina, but I've cooled down now. That's the effect Jim has had on me. I hear he's a plumb peaceful cuss.'

'You get the idea,' Dance smiled. 'Cut out the war talk and if we happen to cross Grindall's trail, you must spout some legal *habla* at him. Maybe a threatened court suit would make him see reason.'

'Well,' Polly laughed, 'that certainly sounds

more sensible.' She appeared greatly relieved.

'Well, let's start walking. We can't stand here talking all night.'

Chuck Osborn started off in one direction. Polly, Dick and Dance took another. For the moment, all thought of Grindall was gone. However, Dance knew that trouble couldn't be avoided indefinitely.

When he and Dick had delivered Polly at her boardinghouse, they headed back toward the main street. Dance suddenly became aware that Dick was leading the way toward the Red Phoenix. For a moment he was about to suggest that they turn around and head in another direction. Then he realized he couldn't direct Dick's actions. The boy might resent that. It would be best to let him go where he would. On such a basis, Dick might prove more tractable in the long run.

As luck would have it, Nick Grindall was again heading toward the hitch-rack in front of the Red Phoenix, when Dick and Dance drew near.

Dick's face hardened. 'There's Grindall now.'

Dance laughed softly. 'He was just getting ready to climb into the saddle when I ran into him before. I reckon he's just got around to leaving.'

'There's no time like the present to tell him what's on my mind,' Dick said suddenly, then raising his voice, he called, 'Hi, Grindall! Just a minute!'

Grindall turned, waiting for Dick and the Dancer to come up. He frowned when he recognized the Dancer.

'You still here, Dancer?' he growled. 'Remember, I only give you twenty-four hours. You'd better start your packing—'

'I already started packing,' Dance drawled. 'Packing Colt ca'tridges into my gun cylinders.'

Grindall commenced to swear, then recognized Dick. 'Oh, it was you called me, eh, kid? What do you want?'

His manner grated on the boy's nerves like salt in a fresh wound. Dick opened his mouth to release an angry retort, then, with an effort, held his temper in check. 'I want to talk to you a minute, Grindall,' he said evenly.

'Hurry it up. What do you want?'

'Don't you think, Grindall,' Dick said, still fighting to keep his tones steady, 'that it is about time you let Polly have some of the profits from the Bow-Knot?'

'Polly, eh?' Grindall sneered. 'Pretending to ask for her so you'll get some money, eh?'

'I'm not asking for myself,' Dick insisted, his words trembling a little, 'but you've got to come clean for my sister.'

Grindall laughed coarsely. 'And supposin' I don't?'

'I'll take the matter to court,' Dick stated. 'We'll see if we can't get some right, then.'

'Take it to court,' Grindall rasped, 'and see

124

how far you get. Your maw's will gave me the ranch. You and Polly don't get it until I die—and that's a long way off. If you and Polly die first, I get your shares. It's all plain, black on white, and any court in the land will uphold me. Nope, that will can't be busted!'

'Mother never intended you to treat Polly this way.' Dick's face was white. 'She never believed you would—'

'Don't blame me if your maw was a fool—' Grindall commenced.

And then, Dick hit him! Hit him with all the force and fury of his lithe young body, backed up by a temper that could no longer be held in check.

Grindall staggered, slammed into the hitch-rack, then went down. A string of vile curses left his lips, as he struggled up, one hand clawing at his holster.

'Draw, damn you!' Dick was saying, his own fingers hovering above gun-butt.

Like a flash the Dancer leaped between the two, his right gun in hand.

'Hold it, Grindall,' the Dancer said sternly. 'Dick, you keep your hand away from your iron. There isn't going to be any shooting tonight. Dick, do you hear me?'

His tones snapped the boy into obedience. He held one gun far out from his holster. Reluctantly, Grindall also dropped his grip on his six-shooter. Dance stepped back, putting his gun away.

125

'That's better,' he said quietly. 'Don't forget your promise to Polly, youngster.'

'That was only for tonight,' Dick grated. 'I'm keepin' it, but tomorrow's another day—'

'Damn right, it's another day,' Grindall raged. 'I ain't going to take on two of you—'

'I'm not asking Dance for help,' Dick snapped. 'I'll meet you any time, any place, Grindall.'

'You're afraid to face my guns,' Grindall snarled. Blood was trickling from one corner of his mouth. It added to the savagery of his snarl.

'I'll kill you, Grindall, sure as hell,' Dick said hotly.

Grindall forced a sneering laugh. 'You can't do it, kid. You know damn' well you ain't a match for my guns. You never saw the day when you could pull faster'n me. You kill me? That's a joke!'

'It won't be a joke when I do it,' Dick clipped his words short. 'I know you're a better hand with a six-shooter than I am, Grindall. I've never denied it. You'll probably get me, but I'll be using a shot-gun! Yes, you may get me, but you won't be able to prevent me from pulling trigger first, you lousy, low-lifed bastard!'

'That's enough, Dick,' Dance cut in. 'You've said your say. Come on, we'll climb out of this.' He tried to urge the boy on his way, but Grindall was speaking again.

126

'I've given Dancer his limits to stay in Carabina,' Grindall roared angrily. 'Now, I'm including you in that same order, kid. Get your damn' shot-gun! And you too, Dancer. I'll blast you both to hell!'

He tried to say more, but the angry words stuck in his throat. For the second time that evening he turned and dashed madly up the steps of the Red Phoenix and disappeared through the entrance.

Dick and Dance watched him go. Then Dick sighed, 'I'm sorry, Jim. I didn't mean to lose my temper thataway, only what he said about my mother—'

'It's all, all right, Dick,' Dance said softly. 'You did what any man would do. And you kept your promise to Polly; you didn't draw your guns. Under the same circumstances, I couldn't have done better myself. She'll be proud of you, son.'

'Thanks, Jim.'

The Dancer had the boy by the arm, walking along the sidewalk. The encounter with Grindall had occurred and been finished so quickly there hadn't been any opportunity for a crowd to collect. The Red Phoenix was behind them now. Dance could feel the boy's body trembling under the excitement through which he had just passed.

After a few minutes Dance said quietly, 'You held to your position like a man youngster, but forget that shot-gun talk. If you ever do meet Grindall, use your iron—like a cowhand should.'

Dick didn't reply. Dance looked at him and saw the boy's eyes were filled with tears.

'Forget it, pard,' Dance said softly. 'Everything's all right now.'

'Aw, dammit,' Dick exclaimed, 'I'm acting like somebody should be wet-nursin' me. But I'm not scared, Jim, honest I'm not. I'm just mad.'

'Sure, pard, sure. I understand. C'mon, we'll drift over to the Cowman's Rest. I understand there's a poker game there every night. Maybe we can horn in and win a few bucks. What say?'

He put his arm around the boy's shoulder. Together they walked along the plank sidewalk. Dance wasn't talking now. His mind was too full of the trouble he felt was sure to break forth on the morrow.

CHAPTER ELEVEN

Hutch Worden glanced up in surprise from the seat at the desk, as Grindall burst through the doorway of their office in the Red Phoenix. Grindall came in cursing, slammed the door, and threw himself into a chair.

'Well, for cripes' sake!' Worden snapped. 'You back again?'

'You see me, don't you?'

'Thought you left for the Bow-Knot—say—'

'I did—but—'

'Say,' Worden interrupted, 'you look like you'd been caught in a cyclone. What hit you? This is twice now you went out to get your bronc. Can't you make up your mind? Who hit you, I'm askin'?'

Grindall swore at Worden. Worden laughed sarcastically, while Grindall went to a bucket in one corner and washed the blood from his face. He came back to the desk, reached across Worden to get a bottle from a drawer. Then he drank long and heavily. Finally he returned to his chair, across the desk from Worden.

'Your bronc must have kicked you,' Worden grinned.

'That damn' kid of mine done this,' Grindall growled.

'Who? . . . Oh, young Dick Loomis. Your beloved stepson, eh?' Worden laughed. 'Ain't you the glutton for punishment? First, you give the Dancer twenty-four hours to leave town, which alone is signing your death warrant—'

'I ain't convinced of that, Hutch.'

'You will be tomorrow, at this time, if you're alive—which you won't be. Next, you let your stepson beat you up—'

'He only hit me once.'

'Your face looks like he'd used a mallet for that once.'

Grindall leaped to his feet. 'Hutch, this ain't

129

no laughing matter. If I'd—'

At that moment the door opened and closed to allow Tracy Chapman to enter the office. Chapman looked curiously at Grindall, then asked, 'What happened to your face, Nick, did your horse throw you? You came running back through the room before like you'd—'

'It was either a horse or a mallet,' Worden chuckled. 'He'll tell you young Dick Loomis hit him, but don't you believe it—not unless Loomis used a bung-starter. I know damn' well, though, if Loomis had done it, Nick would have put a slug through the kid in short order, thus getting immediate revenge and at the same time partly settling certain arguments regarding the ownership of the Bow-Knot—'

'How in hell was I to plug the kid,' Grindall growled sulkily, sinking back in his chair, 'when the Dancer was holding a gun on me?'

The smile vanished from Worden's face and he slowly leaned forward, a low whistle of surprise, mingled with concern, escaping his lips. 'So that's how it was,' he said softly. 'The Dancer, eh? How come he had a hand in it? Let's have the story, Nick.'

Grindall finally calmed enough to relate what had happened.

*   *   *

The Dancer rose early the following morning.

130

The sun was still high when he stepped out on the main street of Carabina and went in search of a restaurant to get breakfast, the hotel dining-room not yet being open. For a short time he considered waiting, in the hope of breakfasting with Polly Loomis, but on second thought decided she would probably have her morning meal at the Morley boardinghouse.

The Dancer was becoming more interested in Polly Loomis than he cared to admit. He felt sure the girl liked him. He frowned as he sauntered along in the bright morning sun shining on the almost deserted street. Finally, Dance shook his head. Leading the life he did, he had no right to ask any woman to share it as his wife. For that matter, Dance had always considered himself immune to feminine charms. Polly Loomis was presenting a new problem to him.

Thoughts of Polly brought his mind around to young Dick. Dick presented a problem also, one that would have to be taken care of first. How to keep Grindall from killing the boy— that was what bothered Dance. Of course, there was the barest chance that Dick might, with the aid of a shot-gun, manage to down Grindall, if he did it in open fight, well, that's all there was to the matter. However, if there were not plenty of witnesses present to present Dick's side of the case, there was a strong possibility of the boy swinging for murder.

'And damn the luck,' Dance growled. 'I as

much as promised Polly I'd see no harm came to Dick.'

He sauntered slowly along, arms swinging at his sides, not far from his gun-butts; brow furrowed with tiny wrinkles of thought. People were commencing to appear on the streets now. The Dancer replied to their greetings with absent-minded nods.

In time, he found a restaurant and moodily ate a plate of wheat-cakes, syrup and bacon, washed down with sweetened black coffee. By the time he had finished and was again on the street, he had reached a decision.

'I just reckon,' he mused, 'that I'll have to look up Grindall and force him to shorten that twenty-four hour limit. That will put Grindall out of the running—providing I'm lucky—and at the same time fix things up for Dick and Polly. Yep, that's the ticket.'

He returned to the hotel, cleaned his guns and carefully examined them, to see that all was in mechanical order. Nodding with satisfaction, he left the room and started along the hall that led to the stairway. On his way past Dick's room he paused and knocked gently on the door. There was no answer.

'I reckon the kid's still asleep,' Dance said to himself. 'I won't wake him.' He listened for a moment, then smiled and went on.

He descended the stairs. On his way through the barroom, Jeff Reed hailed him, 'Hey, Mr. Dance, what's this I hear about

Grindall giving you twenty-four hours in which to leave town? The news is all over Carabina—'

'You heard correct,' Dance replied quietly. 'You aren't worrying about my room rent, are you?'

'Hell, no. I was just wondering if—'

'There's money in my coat, up in my room, if anything happens,' Dance said grimly. 'You'll know, before long—'

'Well, good luck.' Reed looked after him with wondering eyes.

'I'll probably need it. Thanks.'

The Dancer stepped into the street and walked deliberately to the Red Phoenix. It was too early for business. Two men stood talking at the bar in the big room, Hutch Worden and Tracy Chapman.

Without any preliminaries, Dance said, 'I'm looking for Grindall.'

Chapman shrank back from the look in the Dancer's eyes. He didn't speak.

Hutch Worden said, 'You'll have to do your looking at the Bow-Knot, Dancer. Nick ain't here.'

'Don't lie to me, Worden.'

'I ain't lying to you. Nick pulled out for the Bow-Knot last night. I ain't seen him since.'

The Dancer said grimly, 'Grindall and I have an appointment. I sure hope it hasn't slipped his mind.'

Worden shrugged his shoulders. 'I don't reckon it has. Nick is plumb anxious to keep that date. You're some previous, aren't you? Your twenty-four hours ain't up, yet—'

'I'm not waiting for that. There's no use wasting time. Grindall might as well get what's coming to him,' Dance said coldly.

'Sure of yourself, ain't you?' Worden sneered.

The Dancer nodded. 'As sure as I'll be when I meet you, Worden.'

Worden paled a trifle under his tan, then, 'You'd better settle Nick first—if you can—before you start threatening me. Nick is a lot better gun than you give him credit for. I'd hate to face him myself—'

'When will he be back?' Dance interrupted.

Again, Worden shrugged his shoulders. 'Any time now. He usually plans to get here by noon, at the latest.'

'Tell him,' the Dancer said steadily, 'that I'm looking for him. Tell him to come with his guns a-smokin'. Tell him to say his prayers first, if he knows how.'

The Dancer wheeled about, without waiting for an answer, and walked back to the street.

There was something of awe in the glance Tracy Chapman sent after the Dancer's light-stepping, lean-bodied figure.

'Lord,' Chapman whispered hoarsely. 'That man's eyes look right through a fellow. I've never before seen anything so hard and cold and relentless. Hutch, I'm glad I'm not in Nick's boots, if Dance ever—'

134

'Quit your worrying,' Worden snapped. He called to the bartender at the end of the long mahogany counter, 'I'm needin' a shot of liquor and I reckon Tracy is too. Serve 'em up.'

From the Red Phoenix, Dance walked back to the hotel, but he didn't enter. He glanced through the side window, into the dining-room, and was glad to see no sign of Dick Loomis.

After breakfast Dance moved on until he had reached the sheriff's office. Sam Purdy was inside. Dance entered and found a chair. Purdy told Dance that Chuck Osborn was 'around town some place,' he wasn't sure where.

Dance didn't talk much. Purdy sensed he had something on his mind and didn't attempt to draw him into conversation.

The Dancer sat, chair tilted back against the wall, sombrero brim drawn low over his eyes. Smoke spiraled from his cigarette to mushroom against the lowered hat brim and make hazy the steely look in his eyes.

The sheriff cleared his throat, 'What you got on your mind, Jim, this coming fight with Grindall?'

'It's not worrying me—not much.' The tones were lazy.

'It's my duty to stop it, you know,' the sheriff commenced uncertainly. 'I aim to be on hand this evening when your time's up and—'

'I don't reckon to cause you any trouble,

Sam.' Still the same drawling tones.

The sheriff fell silent for a time. Finally, he looked up from a frown of concentration. 'I'm going to get some chow. Mind staying here until Chuck shows up?'

'I'll stay,' Dance nodded. 'Slope along.'

At that moment the sound of running footsteps were heard. The next moment, Chuck Osborn burst into the office. His hat was gone, his shirt torn. The knuckles of both hands were bruised and bleeding. His clothing was covered with dirt.

'What in the devil happened to you?' the sheriff snorted. 'You been drinking tea, again?'

Osborn leaned weakly against the doorjamb, panting for breath. 'I come for a gun,' he said weakly. 'They took mine away, before I knowed.'

'Who took your gun?' Purdy demanded.

The Dancer was on his feet now.

'The mob,' Osborn gasped. 'A mob is hanging Dick Loomis. They took my guns away—'

'Dick Loomis!' Dance snapped. 'What for? What's the idea? What's Dick done—'

'Murdered Grindall!' Osborn jerked out. 'Dick's already confessed!'

The Dancer was on his feet now, his features white and strained. He started toward the door, wheeled and came back, waiting for Osborn to explain more fully. A cruel welt had commenced to swell on one side of the deputy's head.

Dance glanced through the open doorway. He saw men running along the sidewalks. From the end of town, the sounds of a commotion broke in on his thoughts.

'Come on!' The Dancer leaped to action. 'Maybe we'll be able to save him.'

He pushed through the doorway, past the beaten Osborn. Sheriff Purdy left his chair in a single leap, reaching to a double-barrelled shot-gun that stood in one corner.

'And they're taking him out to that tall oak west of town,' Osborn was saying, his breath coming jerkily. 'I done my best, Sam, but there was too many for me. Before I could pull my gun, somebody knocked me over the head and I went down. Worden is headin' 'em, I think, but I'm not sure. Things were happening too fast for me to get the details—'

The sheriff brushed past him, swearing under his breath. His horse stood, saddled, out in front. In a moment the sheriff was astride the animal. He saw Dance sprinting along the sidewalk. Looking back, once, he glimpsed Chuck Osborn following. Osborn had secured another gun by this time.

The sheriff caught up with Dance, passed him at a swift lope. Far to the rear, Osborn was half-staggering, half-running, in an effort to catch up with Dance. He saw Dance vault over a hitch-rack and into the saddle of someone's cow-pony which had been left standing before the general store. This gave Chuck renewed hope. In another minute he also saw a waiting horse and commandeered it.

The three riders tore along the dusty road at breakneck speed, the sheriff in the lead. Dance was riding furiously, bent low over the pony's neck. He caught up with the sheriff. For a few moments the two horses raced, nose and nose. Then, slowly, Dance's pony forged ahead.

From behind came the sheriff's appealing yell, 'Stop them, Jim, stop them! I'll be right behind you!'

Dance didn't take time to answer. Using his spurs, he drove the pony mercilessly. The little beast leaped ahead in great strides. Lather commenced to fleck its withers. Its hide was streaked with sweat.

The drumming of the sheriff's horse fell to the rear, but Dance knew that Purdy and Osborn would arrive as soon as they could. Dance dug in his spurs. A panorama of moving street reeled past. Ahead, he saw dust settling in the road, as though a big party of riders had recently passed.

'Lord!' Dance gulped. 'Let me be in time.'

He was nearing the western edge of Carabina now. The houses became more scattered. Only a few 'dobe huts were to be seen on either side. Suddenly the road swung in a great arc to curve around a deserted two-story frame house. Dance nearly swept the

138

little cow-pony from its hoofs, as he reined it around the curve. Then the country opened out.

Ahead of him, not five hundred yards, a party of some twenty riders had halted in the shade of a huge oak tree. A man was just tossing a rope over one of the lower limbs!

Someone heard Dance's horse, swung around and yelled a warning to his companions. Dance caught their startled expressions as several of the men turned. But he was still some distance away from the group beneath the oak. Preparations went forward with greater haste.

One of the mob led under the tree the horse upon which Dick Loomis was seated, with hands bound to the saddle-horn. A loop, knotted in true hangman's fashion, was placed about Dick's neck. The rope ran from the side of the boy's neck, over a limb above his head and thence to the saddle-horn of another rider who sat his horse near by.

A man had just started to lead Dick's horse from under him, after releasing his hands from the saddle-horn, when Dance drew both guns. Standing in his stirrups, he sent a pair of shots whining above the heads of the mob. The mob members paused, drew apart, then again closed in on their victim.

Straight for the group, Dance rode. The mob's nerve faltered, broke. Several of them scattered wildly to get out of the path of

Dance's plunging horse as he pulled to a halt in a scattering of sand and gravel, alongside Dick's horse. Dance slammed one of his guns back in holster. With the other, he covered the other riders, while he removed the rope from Dick's neck.

Behind him sounded an angry curse. Dance turned in the saddle. A burst of white fire left his hand. The rider, to whose saddle the lynching rope had been fastened, suddenly released hold of his gun-butt and let out a yelp of pain. Blood commenced to seep through the sleeve of his gun arm. Dance shifted back, his other gun out now. The mob backed away, then closed in again, muttering dire threats. 'Keep back,' Dance threatened. 'I'll be blowing you all loose from your horses, at the first move you make. Get back, I tell you!'

At his side, Dick spoke. 'You'd better clear out, Jim. They'll be hanging us both, in another minute. Get out and save your skin!'

'Clear out of here, Dancer,' a man yelled. 'We lynch murderers in Carabina.'

The speaker was drunk and wore the togs of a miner. Dance's eyes ran quickly over the group. None of the would-be lynchers were cowpunchers.

'You fellows had better clear out,' Dance said sternly. 'I'll put a slug through the first hombre that tries to put that rope around Dick's neck again—'

'We'll string you up too,' another voice cut

140

in. 'Get ridin', Dancer. That deputy badge on yore vest don't scare me none. Fan yore tail outten here or I'm shootin'—'

The man's gun was already out, but he was too drunk to hold it steady. Dance laughed grimly, thumbed one shot. As though by magic, a strip of the man's felt hat-brim disappeared in thin air. There came a startled gasp of fear and surprise, as the fellow jerked back, dropped his gun. His arms flew into the air and he started to back away.

A swift drumming of hoofs reached Dance's ears. Sheriff Purdy had arrived. He came charging in, wheeled his horse to a stop at Dance's side, a shot-gun held at a menacing angle under one arm.

'Scatter out of here, you scourin's of hell!' Purdy bellowed. 'Get back from this boy. He's my prisoner. Get going. I'm shore itchin' to send scum like you to Hades on a couple of charges of buckshot!'

The mob faltered, then commenced to break, before the levelled guns of Dance and the shot-gun in Purdy's hands. The arrival of Chuck Osborn at that moment completed the rout.

Two or three men urged their ponies out of the way. The others, slower of thought, backed their mounts to the opposite side of the road.

Chuck came plunging in. Near the first rider, he stopped. His gun rose in the air, descended with a sharp crack on the side of the rider's head. The man toppled from his saddle. Chuck grimly urged his pony between two more riders. The men threw their arms into the air—but too late.

Thwack! Thwack! Again, the gun-barrel whipped down. One man plunged from his pony. The other sank forward on his horse's neck. Like a fury from hell, Chuck charged in among the riders, belaboring them right and left. Squeals of pain rose on the air.

'Chuck! Dang yore soul! Stop it!' Purdy yelled. Finally he made Chuck hear the order.

Chuck glanced around, laughed. He was still a trifle angry. 'I'm just evenin' scores, Sam,' he yelled. 'These skunks bent a gun-barrel, or something just as hard, over my head. They beat me up, took my guns away.'

Again he raised his weapon, spurred close to another of the mob who desired frantically to flee, but didn't dare to in the face of Dance's and the sheriff's guns.

'Damn it Chuck!' Purdy boomed. 'I said to stop!'

Reluctantly, Chuck reined his pony near the sheriff, taking up a position on the other side of Dick.

'Now, you lousy, sway-back cowardly sons of yellow bustards!' Chuck bawled. 'Just try to carry out this lynching. I'll fill you so full of lead you won't hold whisky!'

But all of the fight had been taken out of the would-be lynchers by this time. Except for two who sprawled on the earth, and the man who slumped in his saddle, they sat their horses dejectedly, waiting for the sheriff to speak.

Finally, quiet descended. The sheriff said, 'Well, who started this lynching idea, anyhow?'

For a moment no one answered, then one man with a trifle more courage than his mates, replied, 'Ask Worden. He's the one.'

Sudden exclamations burst from the mob. 'Where's Worden?'

'Worden's gone!'

'What become of Hutch Worden?'

'I thought Worden was running this. Where'd he go?'

'Worden ain't here!'

Purdy called for silence, then, 'So Worden was back of this move, eh? He got you fellows started, then left you to carry his ideas through. A fine bunch of skunks you are. Twenty of you against one boy. Whatever gave you the idea that I'd stand for mob rule in this county?'

'Aw, hell,' one man defiantly defended his actions, 'hangin' a murderer ain't no crime.'

'Who says Dick murdered Grindall?' Purdy demanded. 'I ain't seen any proof—'

'Don't need proof,' one of the lynchers broke in, 'when Loomis has already confessed.'

'Huh!' The sheriff's mouth fell open, though he had already heard Osborn make the statement. He turned to Dick. 'Young 'un,

143

where did they get that fool idea?'

Dick hung his head. 'I did it, Sam. Let's not argue the matter.'

'When did you do it?'

'This morning.'

'You killed Nick Grindall this morning?' The sheriff's voice was sceptical. 'Where did you do it?'

'Out to the Bow-Knot.'

'I'm waiting to hear your story,' Purdy persisted. 'How does Polly fit into this?'

'I've talked enough.' Dick didn't meet the sheriff's eyes. 'Grindall deserved killing. I did it. There's nothing to talk about. Take me up. I can talk better when I've had a lawyer—'

'But listen, Dick,' Dance pleaded, 'we're your friends. You can say what—'

'I'm not saying anything more, now,' the boy said stubbornly.

Purdy started to question him again, but meeting Dance's eye, gave up the thought. The Dancer realized Dick didn't want to, and wouldn't, talk further about the matter at that moment.

Purdy turned irritably away, venting his anger on the mob that sat meekly on its horses before him. 'Yo're a bunch of measly scuts, that's what you are,' Purdy raged. 'If I had the room in my jail, I'd jam every last son of you into a cell, and keep him there until the ants carried him out through the keyhole. Of all the yellow, misbegotten sons I ever met, you flea-bitten sidewinders take the—'

The Dancer laughed softly. 'In other words, Sam,' he observed, 'they aren't a damn bit of good. Now that that's settled, what are you aiming to do with 'em?'

The sheriff considered. Chuck Osborn suggested, 'Let's take that rope and string 'em up, one at a time.'

'I reckon,' the sheriff said at last to Dance, 'I'll just order 'em to be on their way. It's a good idea to rid Carabina of a lot of scum.'

Dance nodded. 'That's good sense. If you arrested 'em, the county would be put to the expense of feeding the yellow coyotes. Order 'em out of town. A few of 'em won't fall for the bluff, but the rest will move on. But wait a minute, I want to talk to 'em first.'

The Dancer raised his voice, speaking to one of the would-be lynchers. 'You said Worden started this. How come he isn't with you?'

The man shrugged his shoulders. 'You got me. I thought he was with us when we started. Then, somehow, I sort of lost track of him. I reckon Worden's liquor sort of fuddled our heads.'

Dance's eyes narrowed. 'Oh, so Worden was buying you drinks, eh?'

'Yeah, he was plumb generous this mornin'. He gave us each a bottle and told us to enjoy ourselves.'

'How long were you drinking before you

started out with this fool idea of lynching Loomis?'

'About an hour, I reckon.'

'You got pretty tight, eh?'

'I reckon you'd call it that,' the man admitted.

'I reckon I would,' Dance said grimly. 'None of you men are cowhands. It isn't natural you all had horses. I'm asking howcome?'

'Why, I dunno . . .' The man appeared a bit puzzled. 'I reckon I didn't think of that before. Anyway, when Hutch said to get the hawsses back of the Red Phoenix, we just done it—'

Dance whistled softly. Abruptly, he said, 'So Worden had horses all ready for you, eh?'

The man nodded. 'Worden said he'd take the girl's horse and come with us—'

'What girl?' Dance asked sharply.

'That Loomis gal—Polly, her name is—'

'What has she got to do with this?'

'Don't you know? It was the gal that brought the news of the murder.'

The Dancer winced and fell silent.

Chuck Osborn leaned across Dick's horse to speak to Dance. 'I can tell you about that part,' Chuck said. 'I'll give you the story later—'

'Polly didn't have a thing to do with Grindall's killing,' Dick cried suddenly. 'I'll stand trial for that killing. But you keep *her* out of this.' A look of fear had crossed the boy's face.

'Take it easy, son,' Purdy said quietly. 'Take

it easy. You'll get a square deal.'

Osborn said, 'The folks are commencing to drift out from town.'

The Dancer glanced toward Carabina. Several riders were in sight. A crowd on foot came farther behind. 'I reckon we'd better get back, Sam,' Dance proposed. 'In another minute we won't be able to talk confidentially.'

'Yo're right,' Purdy nodded. Then, to the waiting mobsters, 'I ought to put you shunks in the hoosegow, but I'm afraid the other prisoners might object to the smell. Pick up yore pards, sprawled there on the ground, and get out of my county. If you ever come back, you'll be plenty sorry you forgot what I said. Drift *pronto*! Savvy?'

Dance was talking to Dick now. 'Did they borrow a horse for you, Dick, or is this your own animal?'

'He's mine,' Dick said wanly. 'I reckon, though, I won't get much more chance to ride him.'

'Don't you bet any money on that, boy,' Dance said kindly.

Purdy heard them talking, said to Dick, 'I'll have to arrest you, son, y'understand. In the face of yore confession, there's nothing else for me to do.'

'Sure, I understand, Sam. I'm not holding it against you.'

Purdy smiled his thanks.

By this time, the mob had gathered their

stunned companions, propped them into saddles and were fading dejectedly from the scene. A rider from town came tearing up, face flushed with curiosity. He was followed by other riders.

'What's the trouble, sheriff?' the first rider asked. 'We heard there was a lynching, or murder, or something, out this way—'

'No trouble at all,' Purdy replied tartly. He jerked one thumb over his shoulder toward the departing mob. 'I'm just exterminatin' some vermin out of Carabina, and Hutch kindly supplied the horses to carry 'em—'

'But we heard that young Loomis murdered Nick Grindall?'

The Dancer cut in, 'Worden told you, eh?'

The man nodded.

Dance eyed him quietly a moment, then, 'Don't believe everything you hear, hombre—especially if Worden says it . . . C'mon, sheriff, let's get started.'

Dance led the way on his pony, through the crowd that came streaming out from town. Behind him rode Dick, flanked by Purdy and Osborn. The Dancer didn't speak again, until they were nearing the center of Carabina. At that moment they were passing the Red Phoenix.

Hutch Worden was standing on the broad porch that fronted the building. A look of disappointment crossed Worden's face, as he noted young Loomis in the sheriff's charge.

'Taking the side of crime against justice, eh, sheriff?' he sneered.

Dance shifted in his saddle, to glance back at Worden. Before Purdy could reply, Dance drawled, 'Worden, where did you ever hear that word "justice" before? You don't know anything about it, hombre, but you're going to—mighty soon. Grindall's gone. Doesn't that mean anything to you? Can't you see the writing on the wall that says your time is coming?'

Worden didn't reply. Dance smiled thinly. He shifted back in the saddle and rode on.

The sheriff said, 'Jim, have you got something against Worden?'

'I've got plenty against him,' Dance replied laconically, 'but not one thing I can put the finger of proof on.'

'You know something,' Osborn charged.

The Dancer evaded that. 'I know I borrowed somebody's horse when we left town in such a hurry—'

'Me, too—' Chuck said.

'—and if I don't return it, the fellow will think I aim to keep it—'

'Don't worry. I'll have somebody take care of it,' Chuck said. 'But you haven't answered my question—'

'Did you ask me a question?' Dance smiled.

'I said you knew something.'

'I hope I do. Chuck, I just get hunches now and then. Maybe I'll know more when Dick

149

consents to let us know what happened.'

Dance eyed Dick gravely and allowed his pony to drop at the sheriff's side. Dick rode on, maintaining a stony silence, his young eyes granite hard on the road ahead.

'Not that I can prove anything,' the Dancer said, 'but—well, Worden knew, somehow, that Grindall was going to be killed. He planned a mob to lynch Dick. He had horses ready, and he was free with his liquor to a weakminded group of hombres that hang around the Red Phoenix. All they needed was some cheap whisky and Worden's urging to set 'em afire. A mob is always like that.'

The sheriff was frowning, slowly repeating the Dancer's shrewd observations. 'Worden knew . . . Grindall was to be . . . killed . . . Worden arranged a lynching party . . . to hang Dick for the crime . . .' Abruptly, excitedly, 'Sa-a-ay, Jim, are you hinting that Worden killed Grindall, then planned to throw the blame on Dick?'

'Ask Dick what he knows,' Dance advised gravely. 'Remember, he's already confessed.'

'Oh hell,' Purdy ejaculated disappointedly. 'Well, climb down, gents. Here's where we stop.'

They had arrived before the jail.

CHAPTER TWELVE

The sheriff escorted Dick Loomis to one of the cells, back of his office, in the jail building, then stopped at the door of the cell, a look of dismay on his grizzled features. The cell was already occupied by a haggard faced man in city clothing.

'Dang it, Chuck,' Purdy observed, 'we haven't an empty cell for Dick.'

'I reckon that won't bother Dick any.' Dance smiled.

But Dick refused to smile in return. 'Lock me up any place,' he said dejectedly. 'I won't try to run away. I killed Grindall and I'm willing to stand trial for it—for murder, if you want to call it that.' The sheriff was looking through the iron-barred door at the man in the cell. 'Damn'd if I know what to do,' Purdy growled.

'Let me go, Sam,' the man in the cell pleaded. 'My wife might be needing me—'

'You should have thought of her before you drunk up all your wages in the Red Phoenix,' Osborn said.

The prisoner shrugged his shoulders. 'I was a fool, I know it, but I just felt like celebrating a mite,' he excused his drunkenness.

'I don't like your idea of celebrating,' Osborn said.

'I won't do it again,' the prisoner said humbly. 'And I'm plumb sorry I busted that platter over your head, Chuck. I wa'n't in my right mind—'.

'Oh, cripes.' Purdy said wearily. 'I might as well let you go.' He unlocked and swung open the cell door. 'Get going, feller.'

The prisoner grabbed his hat which lay on the cell cot and hurried out, profuse in his thanks which the sheriff affected not to hear. Chuck followed the man out to the street to give him a last bit of advice regarding drunkenness, then returned to the cell. Dick was already inside, seated hopelessly on the cot. The sheriff and Dance stood before him, endeavoring to persuade the boy to tell his story.

From the other cells came a buzz of conversation as the various prisoners crowded near cell doors and attempted to hear all that was said.

'. . . and you know, Dick,' the sheriff was saying kindly, as Osborn returned to the narrow corridor that divided the twin row of cells, 'if you want to tell your story in privacy, we can go out to my office.'

'It will be best for you to talk,' Dance urged. 'Good gosh, boy, we're your friends. We want to get you out of this scrape. Maybe you won't even have to come to trial, if we can get things squared around, but we can't help you if you refuse to help yourself.'

152

'I'm not asking any help,' Dick returned moodily.

The sheriff gave a long sigh. 'There's none so blind as them that won't see reason.'

'Look here, Dick,' Dance persisted, 'maybe there are reasons why you don't want to tell us things. Suppose we get you a good lawyer. Would you talk to him?'

'Dammit, Jim!' Dick jumped nervously to his feet. 'I haven't asked for a lawyer. I'm not asking you to do anything for me. Why can't you leave me alone? I've confessed to killing Grindall. What more do you want?'

'Oh, well,' Purdy burst out irritably, 'if you want to act like a blamed fool, we'll just—'

'Wait a minute, Sam,' Dance cut in, shooting a warning glance at the sheriff. 'Dick's not going to act like a fool. He's nervous and wrought up. After he's had a chance to think things over he'll realize he's not being square with his friends, when he refuses to let them help him.'

Dick dropped back to the cell cot, burying his face in his hands. Suddenly he looked up. 'You get the "how" of it, Jim,' he said with a wan smile. 'I'm appreciating everything you fellows are trying to do for me, but I just don't feel like talking yet. Let me think matters over in my own fashion. Sure, I'll be wanting a lawyer, but there isn't any rush. I've got to think things over in my own way.'

'All right, son,' Purdy said quietly. 'We'll

153

leave you alone to think out your story in your own way. When you want us, sing out. We'll bring your supper in later and maybe by that time—say, did you have any dinner?'

Dick shook his head. 'I don't want any. I couldn't eat—now.'

Chuck Osborn put in, 'I've got a couple of extra blankets in the office. I'll bring 'em in. They'll make the cot a heap softer. I'll get you some cigarette tobacco, too.'

'Thanks, Chuck. You don't need to bother.'

'Cripes, boy, can't we do anything to make you more comfortable?' Purdy asked.

Dick shook his head, then, 'Yes, you can too. Let me know how Polly is.'

'You mean,' Dance put in, 'let her know about this killing and how she takes it?'

Dick shook his head. 'No—how she is. She was hurt, you know.'

'I don't know.' A lump tightened in Dance's throat. 'What happened to her?'

'Hurt!' Purdy exclaimed.

'I know about that,' Osborn put in. 'She's not hurt bad.'

'But what happened?' Dance persisted anxiously. 'Did Grindall start something with her—?'

'Grindall didn't have anything to do with it,' Osborn replied. 'Her hawss thrun her. I'll give you the story later. You don't need to worry none.' He looked queerly at Dance.

Dance restrained further questions. Within

154

a few minutes Purdy locked the cell door, and he and Osborn started along the corridor toward the sheriff's office.

Dance stood a moment looking through the barred cell door at the dejected figure on the cot.

'Don't you worry, boy,' Dance said softly. 'Just take it easy. You haven't talked, but I'm guessing at a heap of things. You're showing up like a real man. Whatever happens—I'm for you seven ways from the ace. Don't forget that.'

Dick raised his eyes to meet Dance's. There wasn't any evasion in them now. 'Thanks, Jim,' he said simply, 'but I reckon you can't help much. This is something I've got to see through by myself.'

'We'll see about that. *Adiós.*'

'S'long, Jim.'

The Dancer walked along the corridor to the office, entered, and closed the door behind him, cutting off the cells from hearing range. He dropped into a chair across from the sheriff who was seated at his desk. Chuck Osborn was in a third chair, legs stretched wearily out before him.

'If this keeps up,' Chuck observed mournfully, 'I'm afraid I'm going to loose my taste for tea.'

'You and yore tea,' Purdy snorted impatiently. 'Go drink a gallon of it, then slope down to the Red Phoenix and see if you can

155

find them guns that was taken away from you.'

'By golly!' An expression of anger crossed Chuck's face. 'Things have been happening so sudden, I plumb forgot those guns.' He rose to his feet, but Dance detained him.

'Let your guns go for a minute, Chuck, then I'll go along and see if I can help you locate 'em. Meanwhile I want to hear what happened, and how come Polly is mixed into this mess.'

'She's not hurt serious,' Purdy broke in. 'I was talking to Doc Tustin just before you came in here. Polly's got a purty hard bump on the head, and one rib broke. But she's resting easy, and Ma Morley will take good care of her. She'll be around in a short spell. Doc Tustin has gone to make up a coroner's jury. In a short time we'll be heading for the Bow-Knot, to hold an inquest on Grindall, though Tustin says he don't see much use of an inquest, when Dick has already confessed.'

'You insisted on an inquest, eh?' Dance asked suddenly.

Purdy nodded. 'Things aren't just clear in my mind what happened, seeing Dick won't talk. Think an inquest is a good thing, Jim?'

'I'd have demanded one myself, if you hadn't,' Dance nodded. He added, 'I'm darn glad Polly isn't hurt seriously. Chuck, tell us what happened.'

'I'm craving to get those details myself,' Purdy said.

'It was getting along toward noon,' Osborn commenced. 'I was thinking it was nigh chow time, when I hears a hawss comin' like he was racin' the wind. I looks up and sees Polly is ridin' it. I ain't stretchin' things a mite when I tell you she sure looked scared. White as a sheet she was, with her waist hangin' outten her riding skirt and—'

'Never mind those details,' Purdy scowled. 'Get on with your story.'

'All right, all right, but I'm telling this,' Chuck said testily. 'Anyway, Polly looked like she'd seen a ghost. Instead she'd been looking at a dead man. When she saw me she reined over to the sidewalk. I asked her what was wrong, as she pulled up. For a minute she didn't seem to know how to answer. Then she sort of gasped out, "Grindall's dead!"'

'Anybody else hear her say that?' Dance asked sharply.

'Yeah,' Chuck nodded. 'There was several fellers nearby that had figured something was wrong and had come close when they saw her stop to talk to me. Worden was among 'em. It was just across the street from the Red Phoenix when she stopped. Worden asked her what had happened. I asked her too, along with a half-dozen others.'

'Well, what did she say?' Purdy asked impatiently.

'I'll give you the story as soon as I can,' Osborn snapped. 'It seems Polly rode out to the Bow-Knot to get a few belongin's—a picture of her mother, some trinkets, and so on. I know that's true, because I saw a small bundle tied to the saddle. Anyway, she says she didn't see anybody at the BowKnot when she arrived. She went in the house, leaving the front door open, while she walked along the hall to her own room. Here, she packed up her stuff, then took it out and tied it to her saddle—'

'How did she know Grindall was dead,' Purdy wanted to know, 'if she entered the house and got her stuff, and then pulled out—?'

'Let me tell this, will you?' Chuck growled. 'Anyway, she was just getting on her horse, when she thought she heard a noise out back. She isn't sure on that point though, so perhaps that was just her imagination. It might have been a door swinging, or something. She figured maybe somebody was in the bunk-house, so she heads down there to leave word that she won't be back to the Bow-Knot until things have been settled more satisfactorily.'

'And in the bunk-house she found Grindall's body, eh?' Dance guessed.

Chuck nodded. 'You called the turn. From the way Polly acted I reckon Nick wasn't nice to look at. Somebody had used a shot-gun on him.'

'Shot-gun!' Purdy exclaimed. 'Good Gawd! This makes it look bad for Dick, after what he's said. He threatened to use a shot-gun.'

'Whatever Grindall got, he had coming,' Osborn interrupted. He resumed his story, 'I offered to come down here and break the news to you, Sam, and save Polly the trouble. She thanked me and was just getting back on her horse when some damn' fool in the crowd yelled, "Dick Loomis threatened to use a shot-gun on Grindall last night. Grindall told it in the Red Phoenix."'

The sheriff swore. Dance looked grim.

Purdy said, 'How did Polly take that?'

Osborn sadly shook his head. 'She'd been white as ashes before, but I guess the remark made her mad. I reckon she was set to give that feller a tongue-lashing, from the way she looked. Anyway, she jerked around sudden in her stirrup. The movement sort of thrun her pony to one side, and it stepped into a rut and stumbled. I saw Polly slip sidewise, then grab at the saddle-horn. With that, the damn' horse took to bucking. I jumped and grabbed at the bridle, but I was too late. Polly had been thrun hard before I could reach her. Somebody else grabbed the horse and I run to pick Polly up—'

'Was she unconscious when you reached her?' Dance asked.

Chuck nodded. 'There was a bruise on one side of her head, but I didn't figure she was hurt bad. I saw Chad Pickens, of the Circle-Bar, in the crowd. Chad had druv in for supplies that morning and he offered to take

159

Polly to the doctor's in his wagon. I carried her over to the wagon and told Chad to take her to Ma Morley's while I go get Doc Tustin.'

'Where was Dick?' Purdy asked. 'How come that mob—?'

'Give me time, I'll get to that part,' Chuck snapped. 'Don't always be a-rushin' me . . . Anyway, Chad drove off with Polly while I ran down to Doc Tustin's. 'Course, Doc wasn't in, as luck would have it, and I had to chase around town until I found him. He was playing checkers about three doors from the Red Phoenix, all the time I was looking for him. He started for Ma Morley's. About that time I hears a noise coming from the Red Phoenix. I heads that way. A feller come running and says that right after I left, Dick had showed up and seeing the crowd around, asked what was the trouble.'

Chuck paused for breath and went on, 'Somebody in the crowd explained about Polly finding Grindall's dead body. Dick started toward Ma Morley's, then sullen-like he wheeled around and came back to the Red Phoenix. 'Bout that time Worden accuses Dick, point-blank, of murdering Grindall. Dick hesitates a minute, then says, "All right, Worden. I won't deny it. Grindall had it coming." Leastwise,' Chuck added, 'that's the way this feller I stopped, told it to me. He was running to look for me, saying there was a mob aiming to lynch Dick.'

160

'Who was the feller?' Purdy asked.

'Jock McGraw, that works in the harness store.'

'McGraw's all right,' Purdy nodded. 'Then what happened?'

'Everything—seems like,' Osborn growled angrily. 'I rushed up to that mob that was forming in front of the Red Phoenix. They already had Dick tied to his hawss. I busted in and tried to tie him loose. Somebody got behind me with a gun or a club—and down I went. I was dazed for a minute. When I got up my guns had been taken. I lit into the dirty sons with my fists, but I couldn't make much headway. There was too many for me. Finally I busted loose and come running here for help. You and Jim know the rest of the story from then on. Now we got the confessed murderer in a cell. Where do we go from here?'

Dance looked thoughtful. 'The first thing to do, of course, is to get Dick out of this mess.'

'Dam'd if I know how you expect to do that,' Purdy said hopelessly. 'Dick won't make an effort to help himself. Lord, if he'd only say that Grindall throwed down on him, or something of the kind, we could figure on a self-defense case. But the dang kid won't even say that much. He don't seem to give a damn if he hangs or not.'

'That's just it,' Dance nodded. 'He's acting as though he wants to swing and get things over with.'

'I can't see any reason for that attitude,' Osborn frowned. 'Can you?'

'It's a puzzle to me,' Purdy admitted. 'I'm plumb stopped. Ain't you straddlin' the same bronc, Jim?'

Dance nodded soberly. 'It's a puzzle to me, too, but I'm sure of just one thing.'

'What's that?' Purdy and Osborn asked in unison.

'Dick's concealing something.'

'Now ain't that a deep thought,' Purdy said, with some sarcasm. 'Looks like, judging from his refusal to talk, he's concealing damn' nigh everything.'

'You're barking up the wrong tree, Sam. Dick's admitted he killed Grindall, but that admission was made to cover up the real truth.'

'Meaning?' Purdy grunted dubiously.

'Look here, Sam,' Dance explained, 'how does it appear to you? You and Chuck have known Dick for quite a spell. In the short time I've known him he's struck me as a pretty straight-forward youngster.'

'He's all of that,' Purdy nodded.

'There's not a squarer hombre in Carabina,' Osborn said.

'All right then. Does it seem reasonable for Dick to act this way now? He's not the kind to shoot a man in the back. Even if he did, he'd say so. If he'd met Grindall and crossed guns with him, he'd say so. It's just his refusal to talk

162

that arouses my suspicions.'

'Have you come to any conclusions, Jim?'

'Not a conclusion—call it a theory. How does this sound to you? . . . Suppose Worden knew Grindall was to be killed and had already planned to throw suspicion on Dick? You see, Worden, apparently, had it all arranged to get him lynched. Liquor had been dealt out to a bunch of nit-wits. Horses were already waiting, when the news of Grindall's death arrived. Worden's part in that affair ran off almost too smoothly to be natural. I'm expecting that Worden, or one of his crowd, will be producing some clues that point to Dick doing the killing. That would be the next move in such a scheme.'

'I'll take stock in your story when I see said clues,' Purdy nodded. 'What more is there to your story, Jim?'

'Supposing Dick hadn't done the killing?'

'What?' Purdy said.

'He's admitted it,' from Osborn.

'There's a chance,' Dance continued, 'that maybe he didn't do it. If he didn't do it, he wouldn't know the details. If he didn't know the details he'd have to refuse to talk about it, for fear we might trip him up some place and suspect he was trifling with the truth. He may be stalling for time, until he learns more about this killing himself.'

'But why in the name of the seven bald steers,' Purdy exclaimed, 'should Dick say he

163

done it in the first place?'

'Perhaps he's trying to protect somebody.'

Purdy shook his head. 'Your reasoning is too deep for me, Jim. You say, mebbe Worden knew about the murder. That practically means that Worden engineered it. You can't tell me that Dick would want to protect Worden.'

'I didn't say that,' Dance said slowly, reluctantly. 'Maybe Polly Loomis going out to the Bow-Knot interfered in some way with Worden's plans. Maybe it improved 'em—'

'Great Scott, Jim!' Purdy gasped. 'Are you suggesting that Polly Loomis killed Grindall?'

'I didn't say that either,' Dance said wryly. 'But if she did, I could understand Dick trying to protect her, by admitting to the killing himself.'

Osborn nodded. 'It could be, all right. I hate to think it, but Polly had plenty of excuse for killing Grindall, I reckon. On top of that, Grindall may have got fresh with her, when she was at the Bow-Knot. Maybe killing him was the only way she could get out of a tight. Maybe she saw Dick before she met me with the news of Grindall's death, and Dick had already decided to take the blame.'

'Or maybe,' Purdy said, 'Dick just guessed that Polly killed Grindall, after he heard about it.'

Dance smiled. 'You two are just full of theories, but I reckon they don't solve the

164

problem any better than mine do. Sheriff, let's fix it so Polly and Dick won't have a chance to talk to each other, until after the inquest, at least. Can you do that?'

'Shore. I'll give orders to that effect. Old Tim Farrelly always acts as jailer when Chuck and I are away. I want Chuck to attend that inquest with me. Two heads—three, counting yours—is better than one.'

Dance nodded. 'What time is the inquest to be held?'

'Just as soon as Doc Tustin can gather a jury. He'll stop by and pick me up, then we'll ride to the Bow-Knot.'

'Stop for us at the Red Phoenix. We'll be waiting there when we get through getting Chuck's guns.'

'And that looks like we might have another battle,' Chuck said dismally, 'because I sure want them hawg-laigs. Maybe we'd better have a pot of tea, first, Jim.'

'Save your tea-drinking until after the inquest, Chuck. You may need it to calm down on.'

CHAPTER THIRTEEN

Strangely enough, there was little difficulty encountered in retrieving Deputy Chuck Osborn's six-shooters. When he and Dance arrived at the Red Phoenix, they found Hutch Worden seated on the porch with Tracy Chapman. A few other hangers-on were lounging about the place. The doors of the building were closed.

The Dancer and Osborn ascended to the broad porch. Worden eyed them with a sneer on his lips. 'Red Phoenix is closed, gents, out of respect to the death of poor Nick Grindall.'

'You know damn' well we're not here to do any drinking, Worden,' Dance said. 'Your men got Chuck's guns away from him. He wants 'em back—'

'And I want 'em damn' pronto, too!' Chuck said angrily.

'What do you mean by "my men," Dancer?' Worden demanded.

'Just what I said. That mob you furnished drinks to, before you put 'em up to trying to lynch young Loomis—'

'I didn't do anything of the kind. I admit I gave 'em drinks. Why not? That's good business for the Red Phoenix, to treat now and then—'

'Don't lie, Worden. Those lynchers admitted you had horses ready for 'em.'

Worden shrugged his shoulders. 'Can you blame me if they take my horses? Where are those horses, anyway? You're a special deputy. You ought to know.'

'Your mob took 'em. If you don't already know it, I'm telling you that Sheriff Purdy ordered that crew out of Carabina.'

'Damn them for a pack of horse thieves all you like, Dancer, but don't call 'em my mob.'

The Dancer eyed the man sternly. 'It's mighty strange, Worden, you had those broncs all saddled and ready. It doesn't look right.'

Worden hesitated. 'Well, I suppose it does look sort of queer, but that's not my fault. To tell the truth, Nick owned those ponies—'

'You claimed they were yours a minute back.'

'They were really Nick's,' Worden said smoothly. 'He always kept a bunch, out back, saddled and ready to go. Lots of times fellers come here and want to hire a horse. It's good business to have one ready.'

The Dancer eyed Worden a moment, then smiled thinly. Worden's gaze shifted nervously. 'I hope you're satisfied,' he muttered. 'I can't stay here talking all day. I'm going out to the inquest that's to be held—'

'We're going too, so we won't detain you any.'

Chuck was growing angrier every minute. Finally, he burst out impatiently, 'Worden, I want my guns. If I don't get 'em I aim to—'

'Don't get excited, Osborn,' Worden sneered. He seemed relieved to have the subject changed. 'It's bad for your blood pressure—'

'You won't have any blood pressure a-tall,' Chuck commenced, 'unless I get those six-shooters—'

'Those your guns?' Worden jerked one thumb over his shoulder. On the porch floor, near the wall of the building, was a brace of six-shooters and a pair of badly muddied boots.

Chuck swooped down on the guns, picked them up. 'They're mine,' he announced with satisfaction. The gun he had been carrying he thrust into the waistband of his trousers; his own guns he shoved into holsters.

'I saw those weapons laying out in the street,' Worden lied blandly, 'after you busted into that lynching party, Osborn. I didn't know they were yours, or I'd sent 'em down to you by special messenger. It don't say much for a deputy who loses his guns.'

Chuck flushed crimson, but couldn't find his tongue.

Tracy Chapman laughed nervously. 'Maybe those boots are his, too, Hutch. You didn't lose your boots, did you, deputy?'

Chuck eyed Chapman steadily for a moment. 'Don't get sarcastic with me, you pasty-faced rat, or I'll really lose a boot on that part of your carcass that will do the most good.'

Chapman shrank back into silence.

Worden said resentfully, 'Osborn, there's no use of you bullying Tracy. He was just trying to joke with you. He knows those aren't your boots. As a matter of fact those boots belong to young Loomis. They're clues.'

The Dancer and Chuck exchanged quick glances.

The Dancer said, 'Clues eh?' He eyed the boots with fresh interest. 'Meaning just what, Worden?'

'I'll tell that to Sheriff Purdy when he shows up, Dancer. He's the proper man to take charge of 'em—here comes Purdy with the coroner's jury, now. I don't see any sense holding an inquest when the murderer has already confessed. Howsoever, I aim to attend, just to see there aren't excuses found for young Loomis.'

'Plumb interested, aren't you, Worden?' Dance said ironically.

'Nick was my pard,' Worden returned hypocritically. 'I'm intending to see that his murderer swings for the crime.'

At that moment Sheriff Purdy drew rein before the Red Phoenix. Behind him he led two saddled ponies. At his rear rode Doctor Tustin and the six members of his coroner's jury, each one of the jury sober-faced and dignified with the importance of his position. Tustin, himself, was a wiry, little gray-haired man with a good reputation in Carabina for efficiency and thoroughness in anything he undertook.

'I had yore ponies saddled up for you,' the sheriff told Dance and Osborn, as they walked out to the road to meet him. 'Dance, shake

169

hands with Doc Tustin.' The sheriff then introduced Dance to the members of the jury. Osborn and Dance climbed into saddles.

'I think we should be shoving along,' Tustin suggested. 'It'll be four-thirty now before we reach the Bow-Knot.'

'What are you aiming to do with the body after your jury has viewed it, Doc?' Purdy asked.

'Trombly, the undertaker, is coming out for it. He's starting at once, with his wagon. He'll probably be there before we get through.'

Chapman and Worden were also mounting horses. Chapman had some difficulty getting into the saddle. It was easily seen he wasn't accustomed to riding and, no doubt, had had Worden secure him a gentle horse.

Astride his mount, Worden reined close to the sheriff. 'Here's a pair of clues for you, Purdy,' he stated, extending the muddy boots.

'A pair of shoes?' Purdy frowned puzzledly. 'Them's boots and dang muddy ones at that.'

'Not shoes—clues.'

'What about 'em? I don't want 'em.'

'I reckon you do,' Worden insisted. 'These boots were found in Dick Loomis' room at the hotel. I figure I'm doing right by handing 'em over to you.'

'Well, maybe so. How do you figure these boots have anything to do with the killin'?'

Worden shrugged his shoulders. 'I don't know exactly.' He seemed at a loss for an

170

answer.

'How come you got 'em?' the sheriff asked sharply.

'Well, you see,' Worden explained, 'Nick Grindall was a good pal of mine. It hurt to hear he'd been murdered. When I heard that Loomis had confessed, I figured it might be a good idea to pick up any evidence against him that I could. You know how these murderers are: first they'll admit to a killing, then they'll change their mind and deny it. You know—'

'I know yo're beatin' around the bush,' Purdy snapped. 'I asked how you got these boots.'

'Well, to tell the truth,' Worden answered. 'I hired a feller to go to Loomis' room at the hotel, to see what he could pick up. He brought back these boots.'

'H'm,' Purdy frowned. 'Sort of exceedin' your rights, wa'n't you?'

'Pro'bly,' Worden admitted frankly. 'But I didn't want to take a chance of Loomis' wiggling out of the hangman's noose. Nick was a mighty good pard and I thought a heap of him—'

'You've said all that before,' Purdy grunted. 'How do you figure these boots will prove anything against Dick? Why didn't you take his coat too? He didn't have it on today, so it must be in his room.'

Worden shrugged. 'I don't know if the boots will prove a thing. Anyway, this feller I hired to search Loomis' room, brought 'em to me. For some reason he seemed to think they were suspicious—'

'Bosh!' Purdy exploded impatiently. 'Who was this feller?'

'He was a Mex that was just passin' through. He needed some money, so I hired him to slip past Jeff Reed, the hotel, clerk, and up the stairs to Loomis' room—'

'That story,' Dance drawled, 'sounds fishy to me. How did he know which was Loomis' room?'

'You got me,' Worden shrugged his shoulders. 'All I know is that I paid him five dollars for the job when he brought the boots to me.'

'Where is this hombre?' Dance asked.

'He's left town. I don't know where he went.'

'Worden,' Dance said, hard voiced, 'that whole story is made up out of your mind. It never happened. To make it plain, you're a liar!'

Worden's face went scarlet with anger. He backed his pony and one hand moved as though he intended reaching for holster. 'By God, Dance!' he cried. 'You can't say that to me. I'll—'

'I'll say it again and again and again, Worden!' Dance snapped. 'I don't know yet what your scheme is, but it smells pretty high of skullduggery. You're lying and you know it.

Now, if you want to jerk your hardware, go to work. I'm waiting!'

Worden's features worked with emotion. His hand was already on gun-butt, but he hesitated to complete his draw. Dance hadn't even reached to holster, as yet, but sat eyeing Worden steadily, his face a mask of granite.

After a moment, Worden's eyes dropped. 'I ain't drawin' now, Dance,' he muttered. 'I aim to see Loomis hung for murder, first. When that's all settled and done with, you'll pay for those words. No man can call Hutch Worden a liar and live long to tell the tale. There's a reckoning coming.'

'You bet there is,' Dance nodded sternly. 'And I'm more than ready to start that reckoning on its way, any time you're ready.'

'Come on, gents,' Doctor Tustin urged, 'let's get going. We've plenty to do, and fighting doesn't finish the job. Mr. Dance, there may be something in Mr. Worden's claims. Let's wait and see.'

'There may be, Doc, but I doubt it,' Dance drawled. 'Howsomever, I'm not the only one to be considered. Let's go. We'll do our arguing later.'

The horses moved out to the center of the road and in another moment were loping at a good gait in the direction of the Bow-Knot Ranch.

Two miles out of town, Dance reined close to Tustin to ask, 'Was Polly Loomis hurt

173

much?'

Tustin shook his head. 'The girl was pretty well shaken up, but it's not serious. She'll be all right, except for a cracked rib, in a couple of days . . . You look rather concerned, Mr. Dance. You interested in her case?'

Dance colored a little. 'I'm commencing to think I am,' he returned soberly.

He urged his pony up to the advance of the cavalcade, alongside Sheriff Purdy's horse, and loped on.

The sun was pretty well along to the west when the riders arrived at the Bow-Knot. The men dismounted in silence at the back door of the ranch-house, then made their way on foot to the bunk-house, the door of which was closed. The ranch buildings were still deserted, of course.

'The girl closed the door, when she left, anyway,' Doctor Tustin commented.

Dance nodded silently. He was wondering if Polly would take time to close the door under such circumstances. If she hadn't closed it, who had?

Purdy strode ahead, pushed open the door. The men filed in behind him, and walked rather gingerly around the corpse that was sprawled on its back, a few feet inside the entrance.

No one spoke for a few minutes. The body was clothed as the different men in the party remembered having seen Grindall last. One leg was drawn up rather awkwardly under the body. The arms were flung wide in both directions. It was the face—or rather the lack of it—that caught everyone's attention.

One of the jurors shuddered, 'Buckshot shore is devastatin',' he muttered.

'Dang nigh took all of Grindall's head off,' another one said, with a shiver.

Where the face had been, was now only a mangled, bloody mask. On the floor, not far from the body, was the weapon that had accomplished the gruesome job: a double-barrelled shot-gun.

'That scatter-gun shore ended Grindall's life in a hurry,' a juror said philosophically. 'That's the way life is—here today and gone tomorrow.'

Another of the jurors, a clerk in the general store, shook his head knowingly, 'I remember when I sold Nick that shirt and necktie—it was only about a week back. I told him it wasn't stylish to wear a checked shirt and a plaid necktie. I tried to make him see they didn't go well together. I had a catalogue on hand showing the latest New York fashions, but he wouldn't listen to me, even when I told him it might be bad luck to go against what's known to be best in styles. Well, I guess I spoke true. It was bad luck—'

'I think, gentlemen,' Doctor Tustin broke in, 'that we'd better settle to business. The day is slipping fast. There doesn't seem to me to be anything debatable, under the circumstances, but Sheriff Purdy demanded an inquest, so we'll go through with it. I'm sorry Miss Loomis isn't here, to tell us just how she found the body, but she's told me and I'll repeat her words.'

Which he proceeded to do. The story pretty much agreed with that which Polly Loomis had told Chuck Osborn, and which Osborn had related to Purdy and Dance. Other evidence was presented, mainly relating to young Dick Loomis' threats to use a shot-gun on Nick Grindall.

The jurors looked at the body again. The gun was still in the holster.

'Nick never had no opportunity to draw,' a juror said angrily.

The shot-gun, on the floor nearby, was examined and found to be of ten-gauge, with one shell exploded. The remaining shell was loaded with buckshot.

Finally the doctor looked around the circle of men. 'Has anyone any questions to ask?'

There ensued a moment of silence, then Dance said, 'It sort of looks like the dead man's wrists were rubbed raw, Doc. What do you make of that?'

The jury bent closer. Tustin frowned, examined the wrists. His voice was harsh when he replied, 'It looks to me as though Grindall's wrists have been tied together. He was helpless when Loomis used the shot-gun on him.'

An angry murmur ran through the jury. Osborn and Purdy frowned. Dance was puzzled. 'It doesn't seem to me,' he said quietly, 'as if Dick Loomis was the sort of hombre to do anything like that. Those wrists seem to be rubbed pretty raw—the skin's off in places.'

'Maybe,' Tracy Chapman said angrily, 'Nick was fighting to break loose, when he saw Loomis aiming the shot-gun at him.'

'Proving,' Hutch Worden rasped, 'that Loomis is a dirty coward. He didn't even give Nick a fighting chance.'

'That part can be settled later,' Dance cut in coldly. 'Doctor, are there any other wounds on the body? Maybe it should be examined more completely.'

'I don't see that that's necessary,' Worden said.

Tustin glanced up, a bit impatiently, but acceded to the request. The body was turned on its face—or to be more correct the body was turned over. It didn't have any face. No other wounds appeared on the back.

'Want me to strip the clothing off?' Tustin asked Dance, with just a trace of sarcasm in his tones.

'That's not a bad idea,' Dance replied. 'Take the shirt off, anyhow.'

Tustin muttered something under his breath. With a pocket knife he slit the checked woollen shirt up the back, then did the same with the undershirt, and peeled back the clothing.

By the time he had turned the corpse over and entirely removed the upper garments, Dance seemed to have lost interest in the proceedings, as had the rest of the men. At best, it was a gruesome task, and everyone was glad when Tustin had completed the job.

Tustin procured a blanket from a nearby bunk and threw it over the corpse.

'Pore Nick,' sighed the general store clerk. 'It was me that sold him that blanket, too.'

Nobody appeared to hear the remark. The doctor was talking again.

'Gentlemen,' Tustin said, 'I'd say that Grindall was killed some time this morning. It's a bit difficult for me to state the exact hour, without going into the matter more deeply than I have. That, I do not believe necessary, in view of the fact of the murderer's confession. Some time before mid-morning will strike it closely enough, unless some of you insist I perform an autopsy, or something of the sort.'

Tustin paused and glanced ironically at Dance who was paying but slight attention. Dance smiled thinly then, and said, 'I'm satisfied.'

Tustin turned to his jury, 'We'll go up to the house and talk this over. It shouldn't take long, considering young Loomis' admission of guilt.'

The jury retired to the ranch-house and

178

went into conference, leaving the sheriff, Osborn, Dance, Chapman and Worden in the bunk-house.

'I reckon,' Dance said, 'I'll give a look-see around the yard. We might uncover something.'

'That's a good idea,' Worden said promptly—almost too promptly. 'Sheriff, why don't you get those boots from your saddle. We might find some prints to fit 'em.'

'As I remember those boots,' Dance said dryly, 'they were pretty much muddied up. I don't recollect any recent rain to cause mud.'

'We'll give a look-see around, like Worden suggests,' Purdy put in.

The men filed out, and Purdy closed the door on the still form under the blanket.

CHAPTER FOURTEEN

The men wandered rather aimlessly around the ranch yard, glancing at the earth, though Dance didn't know what they expected to find. There were, of course, faint footprints to be seen here and there in the sandy soil, but none of the prints fitted the boots carried by the sheriff.

By this time the day was nearly over. Already the sun was dropping below the saw-toothed edges of the Fuente Range. Within a

179

short time it would be dark.

Purdy and Dance were walking side by side. 'This is all bosh,' Purdy growled. 'I'm tired of totin' these boots around, and I ain't found any sign.'

'I haven't looked for any,' Dance smiled. 'I'm waiting for Worden to work around to it.'

'Meaning what?'

'Worden found those boots. I have a hunch he knows prints that will fit 'em. It wouldn't look genuine if he found 'em right away, but I'll bet a plugged peso he knows where there is sign that will—'

'Hey, sheriff,' Worden called at that minute, 'here's some sign. Let's have those boots.'

Dance laughed softly and glanced at the sheriff.

'You, Jim,' the sheriff stated, 'are due to win one plugged peso.'

He and Dance hurried over to join Worden and Chapman. Osborn, coming from another direction, was also hastening to join them. Worden and Chapman were standing near a water trough, around which the earth was still slightly wet, despite the day's broiling sun which was now setting.

'Look here,' Worden pointed triumphantly to prints in the soft 'dobe earth. 'Here's sign. Let me have those boots a minute, Purdy.'

'I'll do my own looking,' the sheriff grunted.

He bent down and tried the footwear to the prints in the earth. The boots fitted perfectly.

180

The sheriff rose, frowned. 'They fit all right,' he said slowly, 'but I can't figure what makes the ground wet. Particularly around here.'

'That's easy,' from Worden. 'This horse trough must have overflowed. You see, it connects by pipe to a tank, over yonder by the windmill. Loomis came out here and stepped in the mud. He was probably hurrying to get away, after killing Nick, and didn't notice the mud until later. Then, not knowing what prints he might have left, when he discovered mud on his boots he put on another pair on returning to town. He never dreamed of me getting these boots before he could destroy them.'

The Dancer looked queerly at Worden, but made no comment, as the men commenced following up the footprints in the wide strip of wet earth. They had progressed some ten yards when they found themselves at the corral gate. Grindall's horses and a few other animals were inside the enclosure, the earth of which was hoof-marked and chopped up. At the gateway to the corral, the footprints ceased to appear.

'Well, that's clear,' Worden nodded with satisfaction. 'Here's the way it looks to me— Loomis came out here, put his horse in the corral, then went to the bunk-house and killed Nick. I don't know how he managed to tie Nick's hands together, but we can let that part go. After killing Nick, Loomis came running out here. He didn't notice he was stepping in mud as he ran to get his pony out of the corral, but that's what he done.'

'Looks thataway,' Purdy said moodily. 'What do you think, Jim?'

'It *looks* thataway,' Dance repeated Purdy's words, and there was no small irony in his tones.

Worden's eyes narrowed, then he said carelessly, 'Now that nobody's here, I'll have to send somebody out to take care of these ponies. Probably Nick watered 'em this mornin', before he was killed . . . Well, the evidence seems pretty complete.'

'Yeah, it does,' Dance drawled. 'Almost too complete. It's too bad none of you gents that took part in examining the body didn't see Dick's initials on that shot-gun, too. That, you know, would have made the evidence even more complete.'

Worden appeared to be startled at the news. 'Was his initials on that gun?'

Dance nodded. 'R.L. Stamped real small on the stock, up near the trigger. I didn't think any of you noticed those initials. Thought I'd better mention it.'

'R.L.,' the sheriff frowned.

'Richard Loomis,' Dance supplied. 'Naturally, he gets called Dick.'

'Well, that shore tightens the loop around Loomis' neck,' Worden almost chuckled. 'Being a friend of his, Dance, I'm surprised you mentioned those initials, when the rest of us didn't see 'em.'

'Maybe you'll be surprised at a heap of things, Worden,' Dance drawled. 'You see, friends or no friends, I like to see justice done. Probably at the trial, the gun will be identified as Dick's anyway.'

'I don't know about that,' Worden shrugged his shoulders.

'Maybe you can tell me how the horse trough happened to overflow,' Dance said.

'Must be,' Worden frowned, 'that it just come running from the tank. I suppose somebody forgot to shut it off.'

'And then,' Dance said softly, 'after Dick saw he'd made footprints in the mud, he went over and shut off the pipe flow, eh, Worden?'

Worden looked bewildered. 'Well, he might've,' cautiously.

'Uh-huh,' Dance said, 'but didn't bother to wipe out his boot prints, eh?'

'By gosh, that's right,' Worden appeared to be in a quandary. 'I don't understand it.'

'Maybe,' Dance suggested softly, 'Grindall turned it off.'

'Sure, that explains it—' Worden checked himself abruptly. 'No, that couldn't be. Nick was dead when Loomis left.'

The Dancer laughed softly, 'You don't get me, Worden. That tank might have run into the horse trough and caused it to overflow real early this morning. Grindall shut off the flow.

Then, maybe, a little later, Loomis came here—'

'Of course, of course,' Worden cut in. 'I was dumb not to think of that before.' He seemed relieved. 'That explains everything. You see, there's a valve on that pipe line. The valve is near the tank. It only needs a slight turn to—'

'Uh-huh,' Dance interrupted. 'We see what you're driving at.'

'But what are *you* driving at?' Purdy asked Dance.

Dance smiled, then motioned toward the house. 'Here comes Tustin and his jury. Let's go meet 'em, and see what verdict was returned.'

It was almost too dark by now to see the faces of the doctor and his jurors. Tustin said abruptly, 'Well, that's settled, Purdy. I hope you're satisfied.'

'What's your verdict?'

'The corner's jury,' the doctor said in a sing-song voice, 'after having heard the evidence and examined the victim, renders a verdict that Nicholas Grindall came to his death from shotgun wounds inflicted in the head, presumably by one Richard Loomis. The jury recommends that Loomis be held for trial without bail.'

'Great Christopher!' Purdy growled. 'Yo're shore tough on that boy.'

'Good Lord, Sam,' Tustin said impatiently, 'what else can we do? Judging from those tied wrists, it is brutal, first-degree murder. Loomis

184

has already confessed to killing Grindall. It's an open and shut case, and was just a waste of time to hold an inquest.'

'All right, all right,' Purdy snapped irritably. 'Have it yore own way, Doc. If you want to send that young 'un to the hangman's scaffold—'

'There's no use arguing, Sam,' Dance put in. 'Every man sees things in his own way. Doctor Tustin is rendering a decision as he sees fit.'

'Seems, Jim, like you want to see that boy hang, too,' the sheriff said bitterly. 'You had to go and bring out that fact about the initials on the gun—'

'What initials?' Tustin asked.

Dance explained, then added, 'They would have been noticed before the trial came up, anyway.'

'I suppose so.' Tustin seemed put out that he hadn't discovered the initials himself. He turned away, then asked, 'The undertaker hasn't arrived yet, eh?'

Purdy shook his head. 'Trombly should be along any minute though. That old undertakin' wagon of his rolls along at a right smart gait. If yo're in a hurry, Doc, run along. I'll wait for Trombly. I've got to go back to the bunk-house, anyway, and get that shot-gun. It'll be Exhibit A.'

'I'll wait for the undertaker,' Worden proposed suddenly. 'You hombres run along and get your supper. Nick was my best friend

185

and I guess I can do that much for him. Tracy and I don't mind waiting. Besides I want to talk to Trombly personal and see that Nick gets a nice layout at the funeral.'

And so it was settled. Dance, Purdy, Osborn, Tustin and the coroner's jury mounted their horses and started for Carabina. Worden and Tracy Chapman remained with the corpse.

Three miles from the Bow-Knot, the sheriff and his companions passed Trombly, the undertaker. They stopped only long enough to exchange greetings and tell what the inquest had brought forth, then the undertaker rumbled on in his wagon.

A mile farther on, Dance suddenly checked an impatient exclamation, and dropped behind. Instantly, Purdy and Osborn reined their ponies back at his side. Dance again started on.

'What's the matter, Jim?' Purdy asked.

'I just happened to think,' Dance said slowly, 'that it's not pleasant staying with a corpse.'

'What about it?'

'Worden and Chapman had some reason for remaining behind. Worden isn't broken up much over that body that lays back there.'

'Shall we turn back?' Osborn asked.

Dance shook his head. 'It's too late now. Trombly will be there, and there won't be anything unusual to see nor hear.'

'What did you expect to see?' Purdy asked.

'You've got me,' Dance said, his voice coming through the gloom of night. The three horses were walking side by side. The doctor and his jury were well up ahead by this time, hurrying home to their suppers.

Dance added after a minute, 'I know one thing—water doesn't run uphill.'

'Huh?' from Purdy. 'What are you talking about?'

'When we were looking at the footprints made by Dick's boots,' Dance said, 'did you hombres notice anything queer?'

Osborn asked, 'What do you mean?'

'Well,' the sheriff scowled, 'somehow those prints didn't look quite natural. I've been thinking about that, but I can't decide exactly what was wrong—'

'I know what you mean,' Dance said, 'but I'm not talking about that. We'll go into that later. What I'm speaking of, is that water that was supposed to have overflowed the horse trough and ran toward the corral.'

'What about it?' Purdy asked.

'That water, I'm betting,' Dance replied, 'was poured along the earth, at that point, from buckets. You see, if the trough had overflowed the water would have run in another direction. From the horse trough to the corral it's upgrade. Water doesn't run uphill. Is that clear?'

'Well, I'll be damned!' Purdy exclaimed, 'I

187

never noticed the ground slope there.'

'Me, neither,' said Osborn.

'It doesn't slope much,' Dance responded, 'but it slopes too much for water to run that way . . . Worden is working to hang this killing on Dick. Those footprints were purposely placed there for us to find. When we didn't notice 'em right off, Worden drew our attention to 'em.'

'But if Dick didn't make 'em,' the sheriff sounded bewildered, 'who did? Of course, those boots may not belong to Dick, but—'

'I'll bet a mess of hoptoads they're Dick's boots, all right,' Dance said grimly, 'though I don't think they were taken from Dick's room in the Cowman's Rest Hotel. What makes me so suspicious is the way Worden's ideas dovetail into hanging the killing on Dick. Somehow or other Worden never expected Dick to confess to the killing.'

'What makes you think so?' from Purdy.

'If he'd known Dick was going to confess he'd never have gone to the trouble to make those footprints.'

'Do you think Worden did that?'

'Either he did, or he had it done by somebody else.'

The sheriff's voice sounded hopeless. 'Well, anyway you look at it, Dick is in a bad jam. I don't know how to help him out, either.'

'Neither do I,' Dance said, 'but I'm going to find a way.'

The men loped on in silence. The doctor and his jury were far ahead by this time, but Dance, Purdy and Osborn soon overtook them and went racing past.

Arriving in Carabina, the three at once ate supper, then Osborn and Purdy departed for the jail. Dance didn't accompany them, saying he wanted to loaf around town for a time and see what he could see, which cryptic remark he didn't explain.

Dance went first to the Cowman's Rest Hotel, where he held a brief conversation with Jeff Reed, the combination clerk and bartender. Finally, Dance nodded and departed for the street. In front of the hotel was a long wooden bench. Here Dance seated himself and commenced to roll a cigarette. There weren't many people abroad; nearly everyone was at supper. Yellow light gleamed from windows and doorways along the street.

Dance's cigarette was nearly consumed, when his two Mexican helpers came sauntering along the sidewalk. They didn't stop close to Dance, but idly took up slouching positions a few feet away, against the wall of the building. They too smoked cigarettes. Occasionally, a pedestrian walked by.

Finally, when no one was near, Dance spoke softly, without turning his head toward the Mexicans, 'What news, Pascual?'

The quiet reply came back through the semi-gloom. 'Juan and I went to the Red

Phoenix and tried to secure jobs with Grindall, as you ordered. He refused to hire us, saying if we were friends of Buck Fenell he didn't want us around. Juan explained that we were not friends of Fenell, but it was of no use. Grindall would not hire us.'

He fell silent. Dance pondered. The Bow-Knot should have a crew, by all reasoning. But Grindall had refused to take the Mexicans on. That meant Grindall didn't want strangers on the Bow-Knot. Dance frowned. Why? He had made a thorough search of the Bow-Knot buildings, but without finding what he sought.

Juan spoke again. 'Today, Señor Dance, we hear that Dick Loomis has killed the Grindall hombre. Also, we have heard some talk, from the Señor Doctor's jury, which has to do with the finding of Dick Loomis' boots in the room of the hotel.'

'You heard correct, Juan. What now?'

Pascual took up the conversation. 'Last night, Juan and I saw Grindall ride away from the Red Phoenix—'

'Pro'bly heading for the Bow-Knot.'

'But, Señor Dance, he returned.'

'What! I'm waiting. Go on.'

Pascual remained silent, until a couple of pedestrians had sauntered past, then resumed, 'While Juan slept, I remained hidden for the better part of the night, in that old, deserted building across from the Red Phoenix. Before dawn I saw Grindall return. The Red Phoenix was closed, but the Worden hombre was plainly waiting for Grindall's return, for he once emerged from the doorway, when Grindall's horse stopped.'

'Did you hear what was said?' Dance asked, concealing his impatience.

'Very little. Their voices were low. Grindall did not dismount. I did hear him say, "Here are the kid's boots, Hutch." Worden laughed, as though at a huge joke. They spoke other words I could not hear. Then Grindall turned his horse and rode away.'

'Heading back to the Bow-Knot, I suppose,' Dance muttered, half to himself. 'Well, if Dick ever does come to trial, I'll spike one bit of evidence, anyway.' Then to Pascual, 'What became of Worden?'

'He locked the doors of the Red Phoenix, and walked out of sight along the street. Later, I heard a horse running, but whether Worden rode him, I cannot say. Perhaps he went to his bed. It may be I should have followed him, but I thought it best to watch before the Red Phoenix. If he returned it must have been by the rear way. I did not see him again.'

'It's all right, Pascual. You follow orders to the letter. I told you to watch the Red Phoenix. You've done fine.'

'*Gracias*, Señor Dance. What next?'

'Stay close to Worden, if possible. Hear all that he says, and remember it for me.'

'*Si*, Señor Dance.'

191

The two Mexicans moved slowly off in the direction of the Red Phoenix. Dance watched them leave, then rolled another cigarette. 'If I ever do get this business straightened out,' he mused, 'those two Mex boys will deserve a heap of credit.'

He lighted his cigarette, rose and strolled off in the direction of the sheriff's office.

CHAPTER FIFTEEN

Dance shoved a chair across to Dick Loomis. 'Sit down, boy, Purdy and I are aiming to third-degree you.'

Dick dropped hopelessly into the chair. 'Look here, Jim,' he pleaded, 'there's no use asking me any more questions. I've admitted the killing. Why make me—?'

'We're aiming to third-degree you, to get you out of this mess, Dick,' Dance continued. 'Listen, we know dang well you didn't kill Grindall—'

Dick leaped to his feet, eyes wide. 'I did! I did!' he cried excitedly. 'I tell you I did!' He dropped back in the chair and buried his face in his hands.

Dance saw he'd have to change his tactics if he wanted to get any information out of Dick. Quite suddenly, the Dancer's manner became cold and hard and stern. 'Cut out the baby stuff, kid,' he snapped. 'All right, you killed him. We'll take your word for it. We've got things pretty well doped out, but we want the details. Look at me!'

Osborn and the sheriff looked astonished at Dance's sudden change, but they remained silent.

Dick's eyes met Dance's squarely, his lips a thin line, his chin determined. He was thoroughly angry now. 'All right, Dance,' Dick said coldly. 'You tell me your story and I'll supply the details.' He didn't realize Dance's manner was assumed.

Dance nodded frigidly, spoke brief, terse sentences. 'We went to the Bow-Knot. We found Grindall with two forty-five slugs through his heart. He was laying on the front porch of the ranch-house. He had his six-shooter still held in his hand. Now, if you'll tell us just what happened before you shot him, we'll have the details.'

'All right.' Dick pondered a moment, then started his story in halting phrases, 'I was pretty mad at Grindall, as you know. This morning I got up and rode out to the Bow-Knot—'

'What time was that?' Dance asked.

'I left Carabina around nine o'clock,' Dick said, after a moment. 'Anyway, when I got to the Bow-Knot, Grindall was standing on the house porch. We had some words about the property—the Bow-Knot—and suddenly we both lost our tempers. I don't know how it happened, but I jerked my iron and shot twice. I saw him pull his gun then fall. I turned my horse and rode back to town. You know what happened from then on.'

'It's dang queer,' Dance said softly, 'that you didn't meet Polly. She'd been out there—'

'Oh, yes,' Dick said hastily, 'I forgot to mention that. You see—'

'I see enough,' Dance grinned, 'to tell me you don't know a damn' thing about that killing. You're trying to shield someone else, but it's no use—'

Dick stopped aghast. 'I'm not going to talk any more. I want to see Polly. I want to see if she is bad hurt.'

'I'll take you to see Polly tomorrow,' Purdy promised. 'And she ain't hurt bad.'

'Don't worry, Dick,' Dance said, 'I have a hunch that everything's going to be all right.'

Dance smiled encouragingly. Then he nodded to Purdy and the two men walked to the front door. Dance said goodbye and hurried down the street.

He inquired of a passer-by the directions to Trombly's Undertaking Parlors, then hastened on. At the undertaker's, a light was burning in a back room. Dance knocked on the door which was opened by a tall, solemn-looking man with wispy hair and a long red nose.

Dance introduced himself. 'I'm just wondering if I can have another look at that

194

body you brought from the Bow-Knot this evening.'

'Sure—oh, yes, you're Sheriff Purdy's new deputy.'

Trombly led the way to the back of the shop. 'This is a terrible murder,' he said solemnly. 'It will be a job for me to make Nick Grindall look natural. It simply can't be done, that's all. Hutch Worden was in some time ago. Worden suggests that we bury the body as soon as possible, so people won't have to see the damage that was done by young Loomis' shot-gun.'

Dance again viewed the body, now stripped to the skin. He started to leave after a few minutes. At the doorway he paused and said to Trombly, 'In spite of what Worden wants you to do, Mr. Trombly, you'd better not hold the funeral for a couple of days yet—'

'But, Mister Dance, I can't—'

'Oh, yes you can. I'm asking you not to be too quick with the burial, Trombly.' The Dancer's eyes were hard. 'There may be another inquest held. I haven't decided yet. And don't tell Worden I requested this.'

'But, Mister Dance—'

'Don't buck the law, either, Trombly. I'm not wearing this badge for an ornament. I have good reasons for my request.'

Something in Dance's tones suddenly made Trombly accede to the request. 'Certainly, Mister Dance, if you say so—'

'I do say so.'

'I'll do it. And I won't say a word to Worden. I'll find some excuse if he wants to know why I've postponed the funeral—'

'Sure. Much obliged. You can tell Worden the nature of the wound made the case more difficult to handle than you had contemplated . . . Good-night.'

'Good-night, Mister Dance.'

The door closed behind Dance.

He hurried on. A light was burning in the front window of the Morley house when he arrived. Ma Morley, herself, answered his knock.

'Is that you, Jim?' Polly Loomis called from a room off the hall.

'It's me,' Dance called back.

Ma Morley led him across the hall and opened the door to the inner room. Dance passed through and contrived to close the door after him, much to Ma Morley's disappointment.

Polly sat in a big chair, bolstered with pillows, at the far end of the room. The girl looked pale and drawn. A bandage covered one side of her head. She forced a small smile as Dance quickly crossed the room.

'It's mighty nice of you to come, Jim.'

'I don't dare tell you,' he said steadily, 'how much I've wanted to come. I wanted to call and see how you are. I understood you were to be kept quiet, without visitors, or I'd have been

196

here long since.'

Polly's hand was in his own. After a moment she flushed a trifle and withdrew it. The girl seemed to be laboring under some sort of excitement.

'Take it easy, girl. I understand you have a cracked rib. I hope that knock on the head didn't—'

'Jim, is it true,' she cut in, 'that Dick has confessed to killing Nick Grindall?'

'Yes, it is,' Jim admitted reluctantly, 'but don't let that worry you—'

'Oh, Jim,' Polly wailed. Further words wouldn't come for a moment. Her eyes filled with tears.

Jim sat down on a nearby chair. 'Now, don't you worry,' he commenced. 'We're going to have Dick out of there, plumb *pronto*. You just rest easy and—'

'Jim!' Polly's voice was tense with excitement. 'Listen to me. Dick must never come to trial for that killing.' She half rose in her chair. 'Dick didn't do it. Folks must know the truth. I killed Nick Grindall.'

'Polly!'

Dance leaped up and started toward the girl. A slight noise near an open window caught his attention. Warned by some inner sense, he whirled around.

There, framed in the lower half of the window, was a hateful, pasty face. Even as Dance saw him, the man at the window raised a gun. The weapon belched orange fire and smoke!

Dance leaped to one side, drawing one of his guns as he moved. A burst of fire sprayed from his right hand. The man at the window hurried his own shot, which went wild and thudded into the opposite wall, to the left of Dance. Then he disappeared in the night.

Dance jumped to the open window. To the rear, at the side of the house, he heard someone running. Again he fired, but felt sure all of his shots had missed their mark.

Back of him he heard Polly's sharp cry of alarm. In the hall, outside the sitting-room, Ma Morley screamed shrilly. Footsteps thudded swiftly on the second floor and staircase. Excited voices filled the house.

'I'll be right back,' Dance called to Polly.

He threw both feet over the window sill and dropped to the earth outside. His right gun was empty. He shoved it into his holster and reached for the weapon on his left hip. In the yard, back of the house stood a barn. At the rear of the barn was an alley. Dance glanced quickly through the gloom and about the yard, then he started toward the barn.

A shot roared from the alley back of the barn. The missile whined high over Dance's head. He fired once at the flash, heard his slug thud into wood. Then, further noise as though someone were sprinting along the alley, a banging of old tin cans. By this time, yells filled the air: the whole street had been aroused by the noise of the shots.

Around the corner of the barn, Dance darted. Some distance ahead he could make out a dim form, plugging along, stumbling over heaps of refuse, tin cans, old packing cases. In an instant Dance had taken up the chase.

The dim figure kept ahead of him, but slowly Dance started to gain on it. Crimson fire again burst out. Dance felt a bullet whine past his head. He continued to run, as did his assailant.

'That hombre is sure shooting wide,' Dance panted. 'Still I haven't scored any shots myself yet.'

Lights were springing into being along the rear walls of the houses on either side of the alley. Dance had a brief glance of a man stumbling over a rubbish pile, which was half-lighted by the illumination from a rear window.

The Dancer's gun came up. He thumbed two quick shots.

The shooting brought an instant response. The man ahead stopped abruptly. 'Don't shoot! Don't shoot!' he screamed in terror. 'I give up.'

Dance came up on the run, his six-shooter ready for business. The man was waiting dejectedly, leaning against a backyard fence, his gun hanging at arm's length.

'Drop your hardware!' Dancer ordered.

'Quick!'

He heard the gun clatter on the ground, then closed in as the man stuck his arms into the air.

'Thought I recognized you at the window,' Dance said grimly. 'Turn around. Keep your back to me. I don't trust you.'

'What in the devil you chasing me for?' Tracy Chapman asked sullenly. 'I haven't done anything to you.'

Dance laughed. 'That's a fine thing to say, after you tried to plug me through Ma Morley's window.'

'Me? You're insane,' Chapman replied, trying to put a note of surprise in his voice. He wasn't very successful. 'I don't understand what you're talking about, Dancer. I didn't try to shoot you.'

'No? What were you doing in the alley, Chapman? Do you mean to say you didn't fire on me?'

'I didn't know it was you, Dancer,' Chapman muttered. 'I was walking along, minding my own business. I heard a shot fired. I didn't want to be struck by a stray bullet, so I ducked between a couple of houses, to cut through the alley. Then a shot whizzed past me. I started to run. When another shot came I returned the fire. Finally, your shots came so close I thought I'd better take a chance on stopping before I was hit, so whoever was doing the shooting could see I wasn't the man

200

he was after.'

'Congratulations, Chapman.'

'On what?'

'Your alibi. That's fast thinking. But it's no good.'

'Don't you believe me?'

'Not at all.'

Men were commencing to crowd into the alley. A lantern flashed. Then, Dance heard Sheriff Purdy's voice, followed by Osborn's. The two law officers came shoving through the crowd that had collected.

'Is that you, Jim?' Purdy asked in surprise.

'Me,' Dance replied, 'and Mister Tracy Chapman. I've been rat-catching.'

The sheriff swore. 'We heard the shooting. Did Chapman hit you?'

'I'm not even sure,' Dance chuckled, 'that he came near hitting me, his shots flew so wide. He needs practice.'

'You hit him?'

Again, Dance chuckled. 'I need some practice myself.'

Purdy picked up Chapman's gun which proved to be a snub nosed .38 calibre weapon, then turned to Chapman, 'Well, what's the idea, Chapman?'

'I thought somebody was after me,' Chapman whined. 'Slugs were coming my way, and I fired back in self-defense—'

Purdy snorted his disgust at the tale. 'Jim, you tell it.'

201

The Dancer related briefly what had happened, including the alibi Chapman had offered. When he had finished, 'That's all there is to it, Sam.'

'What's your idea, Jim?' Purdy asked. 'Do you believe Chapman?'

'Not any,' Dance replied flatly. 'He was trying to get me.'

'But listen—' Chapman started to plead.

'We'll do our listening down to the jail,' Purdy cut in sternly. 'What was the idea, Chapman? Did Hutch Worden put you up to doing this?'

Chapman didn't reply for a moment, then, 'Worden didn't put me up to anything. I tell you it's all a mistake. I wasn't even near the window where Dance was fired on.'

'Don't tangle yourself up more, by lying,' Dance advised. 'I recognized your mug, Chapman.'

Purdy turned to Osborn. 'Take him down to the jail, Chuck. I'll be right along.'

Osborn led the protesting Chapman away. The crowd commenced to disperse.

The sheriff drew Dance to one side. 'What's your idea on this business, Jim?'

'My advice is to keep Chapman locked up for a few days. Maybe we'll be able to scare something out of him. I think Worden was behind this night's shooting all right. Chapman hasn't enough nerve to go gunning for me on his own.'

The sheriff looked thoughtful. 'I reckon you've got the right of it. Are you coming down to the jail with me?'

'Not right away. I want to get back and see Polly.'

'Oh, yes. I'd forgotten you were at her place. Did you find out what she wanted?'

Dance nodded soberly. 'She wanted to tell me that Dick couldn't have killed Grindall—because *she* did.'

'Wha-a-at?'

'That's what Polly claims.'

'Good Lord, Jim—'

'Don't get excited, Sam. I know mighty well Polly didn't kill Grindall, only it makes me pretty hot to see her being worried over the doings of a nest of snakes.'

Purdy shook his head. 'Not Dick. Not Polly. Who did the killing then?'

'I've got certain theories, Sam, but until I find out if they'll work, I'm not talking.'

* * *

With the Red Phoenix closed, due to Grindall's death, as Hutch Worden expressed it, the town was much more quiet than was customary. Halfway to his hotel Dance encountered Pascual. There was no one near. They halted to talk.

'The Señor Chapman became too reckless—no?' The Mexican's teeth flashed

203

white in the darkness.

'You know about that, eh, Pascual?'

'*Si*, Señor Dance. I was in the crowd that gathered about you when the sheriff took Chapman under arrest. It was Worden's idea that Chapman try to kill you.'

'Good work, Pascual. Tell me.'

'You remember you said, Señor Dance, to keep an eye on the Señor Worden? Well, Juan and I went to the Red Phonix, but Worden was in his office, upstairs.'

'You went up there?' Dance was slightly surprised.

'No, Señor Dance, not by the stairway.' The Mexican's voice was whimsical. 'Juan—ah, *señor,* he is the devil's own for getting ideas— anyway, it was Juan who suggested that we put up a ladder to reach to the roof of the Red Phoenix. The ladder lay there, at hand, at the rear of the building, waiting for us, as though the *buen Dios* in His so great kindness had arranged all.'

'Yes,' Dance chuckled, 'go on.'

'The open window of the office is near to the roof edge. Juan and I had but to lay on our bellies and listen closely. To our ears came two voices—those of Chapman and Worden. Chapman was ver' much afraid. He has not much of the nerve. He fears you will "spoil everythin', and place him behind bars." Those were his words.'

The Mexican paused to twist a corn-husk

cigarette, then continued, 'The Señor Worden, he loses his nerve a small bit, also, I think. Juan and I hear him tell Chapman how easy it would be to spy on your movements, follow you and put a slug between your shoulder blades. He promises to get Chapman out of any trouble that might follow, in the event he were caught. Chapman is ver' much afraid, but finally consents to try. It seems he has reached the point where murder is preferable to a term in the *penitencieria.*'

'I think you're right, Pascual,' Dance said, patting the Mexican on the shoulder. 'You've been a big help to me.'

Dance rolled a cigarette, held the match flame for the Mexican's corn-husk smoke, then sauntered on toward the hotel.

Behind him floated Pascual's soft, '*Gracias, Buenas noches*—good-night, Señor Dance.'

CHAPTER SIXTEEN

The Dancer slept well, rose about seven-thirty and found his breakfast at a restaurant a short distance from Sheriff Purdy's office. From the restaurant he walked directly to the jail building. Osborn and Purdy were seated in front of the building, their chairs tilted against the wall, shaded from the sun. Their chairs banged down as Dance approached.

'Morning, gents,' Dance greeted. 'You both look like you've got something on your mind, this morning.'

'We've been waiting for you to show up,' Osborn grunted. He jerked one thumb over his shoulder. 'Hutch Worden's inside.'

'You don't mean,' Dance said, 'that you've arrested Worden?'

Purdy shook his head. 'He's visiting Chapman. Chapman didn't sleep well last night, I reckon, from the way he looks this morning. First thing, before breakfast, he starts demandin' that I send for Worden. I refused at first, then Worden showed up here, saying he'd just heard that Chapman had been arrested.'

'The lousy liar,' Osborn put in. 'Worden knew all right. The news was all over town.'

'I wa'n't going to let Worden in to talk to Chapman,' Purdy continued. 'Howsomever, Worden said he'd get a lawyer and I'd have to let him into the jail. Worden said he'd have the lawyer get out a writ of *habeas corpus.* I figured it was better to let Worden in to see Chapman, than to have him bringing in some lawyer to muddle things up. What do you think, Jim?'

Dance nodded. 'Sure, it won't make any difference. You didn't get to hear what they talked about, did you?'

Purdy shook his head. 'Chuck hung around, but Chapman wouldn't talk—or Worden wouldn't let him talk—I don't know which.'

'Anyway,' Osborn said, 'I reckon Chapman was within his legal rights in asking to be allowed to see a visitor. I didn't see any use in arguing the question, so I locked Worden in the cell with Chapman and left 'em alone.' Chuck smiled sourly. 'Course, Chapman being in the outside cell at the back corner of this building, I figured to listen outside the cell window, but I guess they must have suspected something like that, because they started whispering and I couldn't make out what was passing between them.'

'You didn't overhear anything a-tall, eh?' Dance asked.

'Not much,' from Osborn. 'I did hear Chapman say that if Worden didn't get him out, he'd spill everything he knew. Worden sort of hushed him up, and promised to get him out within a few days. About that time they started whispering and I couldn't hear anything more.'

Dance nodded. 'How about Dick? Did you tell him—?'

Purdy broke in, 'I gave Dick his breakfast, here, in my office, and told him the whole story. He owned up that he made that confession because he thought he was protecting Polly.'

At that moment Hutch Worden's voice was heard from the jail; Worden wanted to be released from Chapman's cell.

Purdy sighed. 'I sure wish we could keep that scut in there, but you'd better go let him out, Chuck.'

Osborn rose and entered the building. Within a few minutes he returned with Worden at his heels. Worden scowled at Dance then turned to Purdy, 'When you going to let Tracy out of your jail, Purdy?'

'I ain't yet decided, Hutch,' the sheriff said coldly, 'whether I'll ever let him out. You'd better talk to Dance about that.'

Worden swung around to face Dance. 'Oh, you're the one responsible for holding Tracy, eh? I don't get the idea. You ain't got nothing on him.'

'Nothing a-tall—except that he tried to kill me last night.'

'Hell's bells, Dancer! You got that all wrong. Tracy told me how it was. He heard somebody shooting and fearing to get hit by a stray slug, he cut down that alley. You made a mistake and took after him. Shucks! You're all wrong. Tracy wouldn't hurt a flea.'

'Unless he was put up to said hurting by the sort of skunks that fleas live on, eh, Worden?'

'What are you hinting at, Dancer?'

'I'm not hinting. I'm stating facts I have proof of. You put Chapman up to trying to kill me. He didn't have any luck. It must be, Worden, you're losing your nerve, when you have to have somebody else do your killing.'

Worden forced a laugh. 'I've never heard of

anything so crazy in my life, Dancer. You must be dreaming. Why should I put Tracy up to bumping you off?'

'Think it over, Worden. Any time I'm pushed, I'll produce that proof I mentioned. Yes, you've had plenty reason to want me killed. What's more, you're going to have additional reasons before long. Let's face the facts, Worden. We're out to get each other, and we both know it.'

Worden paled. 'Aw, you haven't anything on me, Dancer. My conscience is clear—'

'Clear rotten, you mean—'

Worden stiffened. 'Don't you crowd me, Dancer. I won't take—'

'You'll take exactly what I hand you,' Dance snapped, 'or jerk your hardware. Which do you want?'

Worden shook his head, sneered, 'I'm not afraid of you, Dancer, not by a damn' sight, but I refuse to run chances of being wounded until I've seen young Loomis hang for killing poor Nick Grindall. The evidence will convict him—'

'What evidence?' Dance said coldly.

'The threats he made to use a shot-gun on Nick. It was his gun. Best of all, those footprints in the mud—'

Dance swore impatiently. 'Those footprints aren't worth a damn, Worden . . . Sheriff, you remarked there was something queer-looking about those prints out to the Bow-Knot. Have you decided just yet what it was?'

'I've been thinking about that,' Purdy frowned. 'It seems to me those prints were wider than they should have been and awful deep near the toes.'

'That's it,' Dance nodded. 'You remember what they looked like, don't you?'

'As well as if I had a picture of 'em before me,' Purdy nodded promptly.

'I'll tell you what made that "sign" look thataway,' Dance went on. 'Those prints were made by Dick's boots—but Dick wasn't in them at the time—'

'Aw, you're crazy,' Worden growled uneasily.

Dance disregarded the remark. He continued, to Purdy, 'The hombre that wore Dick's boots to make those prints, had feet a good bit larger than Dick. He was a heavier man. That threw his weight down into the toes and made the toe prints deeper than normal. At the same time his feet spread out in the soft leather and made a sign that was unusually wide, beyond the mark of the sole.'

Worden swore suddenly. 'I've never heard of anything so cuckoo.'

Purdy whirled fiercely on Worden. 'That's enough out of you,' he bellowed. 'I'm through fooling around with you. You're under arrest!'

'Me, what for?' Worden laughed sarcastically.

'For the murder of Nicholas Grindall!' Purdy stated dramatically. 'Will you come quiet, or have I got to fill you full of lead?'

'Have you gone crazy, too?' Worden snarled, backing away. 'You ain't got no proof against me. You're just trying to find a loophole for young Loomis to wiggle through.'

The sheriff's gun was out. 'Stick 'em up, you measly scut. You're under arrest, and I don't want any back talk.'

'Just a minute, Sam,' Dance cut in. 'I reckon yo're a mite premature, aren't you?'

Purdy turned disappointedly to Dance. 'Huh? Well, if he didn't kill Grindall, who did?'

'Loomis, of course,' Worden growled. 'You can't hang that murder on my doorstep.'

'Loomis has confessed, hasn't he?' Dance pointed out.

The sheriff suddenly relaxed. 'All right,' he said to Worden, 'you get to hell away from my office, or I'll arrest you for loitering.'

Worden swore under his breath, but made haste to retreat rapidly down the street. Disgruntled, Purdy turned to Dance. Dance was laughing softly. Osborn and Dick were just disappearing inside the jail building.

'What's got into you?' Purdy demanded.

Dance grinned. 'Sort of lost your temper and jumped to conclusions, didn't you, Sam?'

The sheriff smiled ruefully. 'I reckon I did, Jim, but that measly son of perdition makes me mad. I'll jail him yet for that murder.'

'Let him run loose a spell,' Dance advised.

'Give him enough rope and he'll hang himself.'

'I reckon you're right,' Purdy nodded reluctantly, 'but I'm sure honing for some action in this case. We know Dick ain't guilty, and so Worden must be—'

'Maybe I'll have news for you by evening,' Dance said.

CHAPTER SEVENTEEN

Dance pulled his horse to a halt in the ranch yard of the deserted Bow-Knot outfit. He dismounted, led the pony to the horse trough and watered it. The prints made by Dick's boots were still plain in the dried mud. Dance glanced swiftly around. His gaze went toward the ranch-house. That extra sense that some men possess was working frantically now, to warn him of—what? Dance couldn't decide. He tethered the pony near the trough, then made his way on foot toward the ranch-house.

Struck by a new thought he stepped outside and made his way back to the water trough. The pony whinnied at his approach, but Dance didn't even hear it now. He was too intent on following the prints made in the mud by Dick's boots—boots worn by a larger man than Dick, however.

Straight to the corral the prints led Dance. He didn't scrutinize them closely until he had nearly reached the corral gate. Then he bent near to the earth, noting the direction in which the last print pointed.

From the ground, Dance glanced toward the lower bar of the corral. His heart leaped as he found what he sought—a tiny trace of mud still stuck to that lower bar of the corral fence.

Higher up on the next bar was another smudge of mud. Two feet farther along was a third trace of the dried adobe earth. 'That's what happened,' Dance slowly pictured the scene in his mind. 'The hombre who wore Dick's boots to make tracks, stepped from the ground up to this corral fence, then worked his way along the fence to—where?' Dance paused, then, 'I reckon I'll see what I can discover.'

He walked slowly around the corral, noticing that bits of dried mud appeared at regular intervals, where the unknown man had stepped along the corral fence bars. Suddenly, the marks disappeared, only to reappear on a still higher bar. But from that point on, they didn't appear again.

'Looks like,' Dance mused, 'the hombre who wore Dick's boots took wings at this point and flew away.'

He rolled a cigarette and leaned back against the corral fence, smoking thoughtfully, his eyes on the earth. Suddenly he stooped down. Here was another imprint made by a larger boot than Dick's. The impression was so faint that none but a skilled reader of 'sign' would ever have noticed it. Not far from this first print was a second one—though this showed little more on the hard-baked earth, than a curved, moon-shaped impression of heel.

'So that's what he did, eh?' Dance muttered, slowly reconstructing the scene in his mind. 'He put on Dick's boots and carried his own. After he had made the prints in the wet mud he stepped to the lower corral bar, and worked his way along the fence, off the ground, until he got around to here. Then he climbed higher and sat on the top bar where he took off Dick's boots and put on his own. Then he jumped down to the earth. Fairly clever, at that. I was just lucky finding these prints he made with his own boots on. Well, I reckon I'll see where these new tracks lead, if possible.'

He stooped low and commenced to follow the faint marks on the hard earth. There wasn't much to follow—a stone loosened here, or a bit of earth scuffed up there; now and then a scarcely discernible impression of a heel.

Suddenly, Dance glanced up, then straightened to full length. The prints were leading him straight toward the big barn. A frown crossed his face. The barn door was standing slightly open.

'Seems like,' Dance muttered, 'I remember closing that door. I might not have, though.'

Impulsively, he left the tracks and started directly toward the barn, which still lay some twenty yards away. Something whined viciously past his face. At the same instant the roar of a six-shooter sounded from the barn!

The Dancer's guns spurted lead and flame as he leaped forward. He didn't expect to hit anyone, but had unleashed his lead to cover his approach. Abruptly, the barn door was slammed shut. The Dancer swerved to one side to get out of range of the crack through which he had observed smoke curling, and from which point his assailant's shots had come.

Silence fell. The Dancer was close to the barn now. He thought he heard movements inside, but he wasn't sure. There were no more shots. He swiftly plugged out his empty shells and replenished his cylinders with fresh cartridges. Once more he closed in, eyes and ears alert for the first sign of the enemy.

None came. Dance reached the door. It was fastened from the inside, but not too tightly to prevent his securing a grip on the edge of the wood. Impatiently, the Dancer bolstered his guns, seized the edge of the door and jerked hard. For a moment it resisted his efforts, then a sudden muscular movement ripped loose the inside fastening hook. The door swung open.

The Dancer's guns were in his hands again. For just a second he paused, then he stepped inside and dodged quickly to one side. A

215

puzzled look crossed his face and he lowered his guns. There wasn't a soul to be seen.

'Damn'd if this isn't queer. This place is empty!'

The Dancer's gaze went swiftly around the big building, seeking another door in the back wall, but there was none to be seen. To the left of the door by which he had entered there was a pair of huge double doors, but these were barred from the inside.

Except for some old harnesses hanging on a peg in one corner the barn was empty. Even the loft was gone; Dance could see clearly to the roof rafters. Hay lay scattered about the floor.

The Dancer listened intently. Could he hear a man's heavy breathing, or was it just his imagination? At any rate he couldn't locate the faint sound.

His gaze ranged around the roof and four walls and hay-strewn floor. That hay gave him an idea. After all, there was no particular reason why that hay should be scattered about the floor, at that season of the year, at least.

And then, while his eyes relentlessly searched, he found one spot where there was less hay than covered the remainder of the floor. That explained things—a trap-door in the floor of the barn!

The Dancer leaped forward, fingers searching the floor for the edges of the trap-door. He found it, fitted smooth and flush with the floor boards. He heard someone fumbling below, evidently trying to lock the trap-door. With a sudden jerk, the Dancer ripped it open. The door fell back with a bang, leaving an opening a yard square. From below came hurried, retreating footsteps!

Two shots roared. Leaden missiles of death flew wide through the opening. Dance hesitated but an instant. There was a ladder leading to the room below, but he scorned to use it. With both guns drawn he leaped down through the opening.

Down he went, dropping, catlike, on the balls of his feet. Landing, he whirled. There was no one to be seen for a moment. In the light from above he made out chairs and a table at one wall. A long bench stood near another. The walls of the underground chamber were built of sandstone. But Dance had no time to notice such details for long. He was looking for his unknown assailant.

From beneath the table came a streak of orange fire. The Dancer felt something hot sear the inner side of his left arm. Then, his own guns were jerking madly in his hands, as he thumbed shot after shot under the table.

There was a scream of agony and then—and then *Nick Grindall staggered into view!*

The Dancer exclaimed triumphantly, 'I knew it.'

The words were drowned in the roaring of guns as Grindall tried a last attempt. But the

Dancer's slugs had already ripped deep holes in Grindall's body. He went down with a crash.

Gun poised for another shot, the Dancer waited. No further movement came from Grindall. His eyes were half open. His lips tried to form words but no sound came. He lay, half-lifted on one elbow, his chest suddenly stained crimson.

Smoke drifted lazily in the under-floor room, essaying to escape from the opening above. An oil lamp suspended on one wall, over the bench, burned hazily in the gray fog of burnt powder. The Dancer suddenly felt very weary. The chase was nearly over. He was suddenly conscious of slight pain in his left arm. It felt warm and damp.

He looked down, laughing grimly. 'Scratch, I reckon—damned lucky scratch.'

Methodically, he reloaded the dead chambers in his cylinders. There was some slight movement from Grindall. The Dancer saw a bottle of whisky on the table. In a moment he had forced a few drops down Grindall's throat. While he waited for a response he glanced around the room. Certain tools on the bench against the far wall caught his eye. He nodded with satisfaction. That's what he was looking for. There should be paper, too, and colored inks, and—

'Dance,' Grindall whispered hoarsely.

'Yes,' came the grim assent, 'are you ready to talk now, Grindall? Time's burning fast.'

'I'll—I'll talk—Dancer.'

Dance made the dying man as comfortable as he could, then settled to listen to his last words . . .

CHAPTER EIGHTEEN

It was nearly dark when Dance rode into Carabina. He headed straight for the sheriff's office. Osborn and Purdy were seated inside, talking, when he arrived. He dismounted, strode through the open doorway and dropped into a chair.

'Howdy, gentlemen.'

Osborn was the first to notice the bandanna wrapped about Dance's left arm. 'What's wrong, Jim? You wounded?'

'It's a little more than a scratch. It stopped bleeding long ago.'

'Who in Hades done it—?' Purdy commenced.

'Close the door and I'll tell you a story,' Dance cut in.

Osborn closed the front door and the one leading to the jail corridor. 'We're waiting to hear,' he said.

Dance smiled grimly, then exploded his bomb. 'This wound was given to me by Nick Grindall.'

For a moment the other two men just stared

219

at him. Then, Purdy said, 'You mean Hutch Worden.'

The Dancer shook his head. 'I said, Grindall.'

'You're plumb loco,' Osborn said. 'Maybe we'd both better have a cup of tea.'

'I believe you have gone crazy, Jim,' Purdy said anxiously. 'I'd like to hear that name once more, to see am I hearing correct.'

'Nick Grindall,' Dance smiled grimly. 'Does that suit you?'

'Then who's that lyin' in the funeral parlor?' Purdy gasped.

'A man named Frank Newport.'

'I don't know him.'

'Look here, Jim,' Osborn cut in, 'did you know all the time that body wasn't Grindall's?'

'I thought it was Grindall, at first, but before the examination was finished, I knew it was Frank Newport.'

'For Gawd's sake,' the sheriff exclaimed, 'give us the story from beginning to end. Keep me waiting much longer and you'll have a nervous wreck on your hands.'

'Two nervous wrecks,' Osborn corrected. 'One of 'em needing gallons of hot tea.'

'Maybe you'll tell us, too, Jim, what brought you to Carabina,' Purdy added.

For reply, Dance brought out a small gold badge which he showed to the two men.

Purdy gave a gasp of surprise. 'Good Lord, Jim, you a member of the U. S. Secret

Service?'

'Division of the Treasury,' Dance nodded, replacing his badge in his pocket.

'That means—' Purdy commenced.

'Counterfeiting,' Dance supplied the word.

'But who—what—' Osborn stammered helplessly.

'I'll get to the story,' Dance said. 'I'll cut it as short as possible because I've still got Worden to pick up. Here's the layout. A year back, Frank Newport—who was also in the service—and I were detailed to find the source of the phony five- and ten-dollar bills that are flooding this part of the country. The two of us scoured the state pretty thoroughly. The search commenced to narrow down to Carabina. I came here, expecting to meet Frank Newport. I learned he'd been here and left.'

'I remember that Newport fellow now,' Purdy said. 'He let on to be a cattle buyer. Stayed at the hotel a short time, then went to stay at the Bow-Knot. Later, Grindall gave it out that Newport had left.'

'Where Grindall made his mistake,' Dance said quietly, 'was in telling it around that he had loaned Newport a horse. I smelled something fishy, right there, because Newport is from the east—Washington sent him from New York to help me—and he never could ride. He always preferred to move by train or wagon.'

Dance paused to roll and light a cigarette, then continued, 'I've got Grindall's confession, to help me explain what happened.'

'Grindall was a counterfeiter, then?' Purdy asked.

'Chapman was the actual counterfeiter. He'd served a term for forgery, and then branched off to making phony money. While he was in prison he became acquainted with Worden. Anyway you understand that Worden, Grindall and Chapman provided the source of the bad money. The money was made in an underground room, under that big barn, at the Bow-Knot. That's where I discovered Grindall—'

'No wonder those skunks always had plenty of money,' Purdy growled. 'But go on, I'm interruptin'.'

'On a pretence of looking for cattle to buy,' Dance went on, 'Newport went to stay at the Bow-Knot for a few days. They made him a prisoner and kept him under the barn. They didn't know what to do with him, but they didn't dare let him go. He'd managed to work the thongs from his wrists a couple of times and nearly escaped.'

'That explains the skin off'n the wrists of the corpse we thought was Grindall,' Osborn put in.

Dance nodded. 'That explains it, Chuck. Well, about that time I arrived in Carabina. You know most of the happenings that took place since then. Grindall was having trouble trying to scheme Polly and Dick out of the Bow-Knot. Then, Grindall lost his head and gave me twenty-four hours to get out of town. Later, he realized he'd made a fool move, but he didn't know how to get out of it, then. On top of that, Dick had threatened him with a shot-gun. Both Grindall and Worden were worried by that time, regarding what to do with Newport. Finally, they decided to murder him. He was pretty much Grindall's build. Grindall held a gun on Newport, made him exchange clothes—then used the shot-gun. He had already signed Newport's name to a note to Jeff Reed, saying Newport was leaving—'

'The dirty, killing coyote!' Purdy burst out.

Osborn was voicing futile, enraged oaths.

'Then,' Dance said, 'they planned to frame Dick for murder, pretending that Newport's body was Grindall's. The nature of the shot-gun wound made it impossible to recognize the features of the corpse.'

'It sure did look like Dick would swing for murder too,' Purdy said.

'The dirty buzzards,' Osborn swore. 'If they could have had Dick executed for murder, there'd been only Polly left with a claim to the Bow-Knot, and Grindall would have got her out of the way, somehow.'

'But how did you know,' Purdy persisted, 'that that was Newport's body instead of Grindall's?'

223

'I didn't, at once. Then I noticed a mark on one finger, where the flesh looked whiter than the rest of the hand. I remembered that Newport had worn a heavy seal ring on that same finger. That started me thinking. I asked the doctor to strip off his shirt. Then, my idea was confirmed. Low-down, partly hidden under the waistband of Newport's pants, was an old scar made by some Italian knife in the east, years ago. Newport pointed it out to me once. To you fellows it was hardly noticeable, but I was looking for it.'

From that point on, Dance related the events that had taken place from the time he arrived at the Bow-Knot, that day, and concluded, 'before Grindall died he made a confession of the whole business.'

'But what was to have become of Grindall?' Osborn asked. 'I mean, in case you hadn't discovered the scheme—?'

'He and Worden hadn't yet worked out that part of the plan, except that Grindall was to stay in hiding until Dick had been hanged for murder. After that, Grindall could show up some day and claim loss of memory or some such ailment to explain his absence. He could pretend he had just wandered away and forgotten who he was. The other body—Newport's—would go down in history as one of these unsolved crimes you read about. Worden and Grindall figured that in a short time the whole affair would be forgotten.'

At that moment there came a rush of footsteps and Polly staggered into the office. 'Jim, Jim!' she half-sobbed. 'Oh, you're safe!'

Dance caught the girl, held her in his arms. 'Of course I'm safe,' he said gently. 'Why not? Good Lord, girl, you shouldn't be out. You're not strong enough yet. Your cracked rib will be—'

'They tried to stop me,' Polly panted, 'but I slipped out of the house. Haven't you heard yet? It's all over town—'

'Heard what?' Dance eyed the girl anxiously in the light of the only lamp Osborn had lighted.

'Worden announced half an hour ago he was going to shoot you on sight,' Polly cried. 'He's been drinking. I was afraid I might be too late to warn you. I wasn't sure if you were here.'

The Dancer laughed softly. 'Don't you get to fretting, honey. There isn't a thing to fear. Worden is talking through his hat. Chuck and I are on our way to arrest him, now. He won't resist two of us. You stay here with Sam. I've just told him a story you'll be interested to hear. Dick can come out and listen, too. But, don't worry.'

'Worden claims,' the girl stated, 'that you're afraid to face his guns.'

'I probably am,' Dance smiled gravely. 'That's why I'm taking Chuck to help in the arrest. There's nothing for you to fear. You see—'

An excited citizen suddenly appeared in the doorway. 'Sheriff,' he panted, 'Worden is on a rampage. Claims he's going to clean out the whole town—'

'Yeah,' Purdy nodded carelessly, 'we heard about it, Bert. Don't let it fret you none.'

The man disappeared from the doorway. Dance lowered Polly into a chair. 'You stay here with Sam while Chuck and I make this arrest; I'll be right back.'

'You promise?' the girl's voice was pleading.

'I promise,' Dance said, meeting her eyes. He turned to the deputy, 'Cmon, Chuck. We'll pick up Worden and put him behind bars.'

Dance left the office, Chuck Osborn at his heels. Neither man spoke as they walked down the street and into the Red Phoenix.

Worden was standing just inside the doorway.

'So you came at last, did you?' Worden sneered. 'You interferin' son, I didn't think you had the nerve—'

The Dancer was tight-lipped. 'Put up those guns, Worden,' he ordered sternly. 'You're under arrest.'

Worden opened his mouth in a scornful guffaw. He swayed slightly, but the rest of his body was as solid as a rock. 'Under arrest! Ho-ho-ho! And for what?'

'Accomplice in the murder of Frank Newport,' the words cracked like rifle shots.

'That's one charge—'

'Murder of who?' Worden steadied himself.

'Frank Newport. You know who I mean. Grindall is dead—but he confessed first, Worden.'

A cunning gleam had come into Worden's eyes. He backed away a few feet. The Dancer followed him relentlessly into the big room. Worden had dropped into a half-crouch now. 'Certainly, Grindall is dead,' he rasped. 'We all know that—'

'I killed him this afternoon—under the barn.'

An oath left Worden's lips. His guns flashed up. The Dancer spun on one foot, carrying himself to one side. His hands flashed to holsters.

Streaks of orange-white crossed and crisscrossed in the big room. The Dancer's left gun was empty now, his right was still roaring. Slugs of hot lead whined all about him.

Worden paused in midstride, his body twisting queerly to one side. The impact of the Dancer's bullets spun him twice around. Then, quite suddenly, Worden's body jackknifed and he pitched, face down, on the floor. His booted toes drummed a convulsive tattoo for a moment, before he lay motionless.

The Dancer took three quick steps and looked down at the dead man. 'I reckon that's all,' he said, half-aloud.

Chuck Osborn appeared in the doorway, a

gun in either hand. He stopped when he saw Worden's still form.

'You were fast enough for him, Jim,' Chuck said.

'I was fast enough,' the Dancer nodded grimly.

He and Osborn descended the steps to the sidewalk. From the crowd on the street arose a sudden, roaring cheer.

When they arrived at the sheriff's office, Sam Purdy was on the sidewalk, smiling gravely at their approach.

'We already know, Jim,' the sheriff said. 'Two fellers run ahead of you to bring us the news. Go in. Polly's waiting.'

The Dancer nodded, brushed past toward the door of the office. Dick stood there smiling. Dance touched his hand as he passed. Inside, Polly waited. Dance went to her. The crowd on the street was still cheering.

'Jim!' Just the one glad cry from the girl. Her lips raised to meet his. His arms closed about her.

After a time, it seemed he could no longer hear the cheering crowd on the street . . .